Mary Burns is travel[ling with] friends when war resum[ed in] 1803 and Napoleon ord[ered] jects on French territor[y]. Captain Armand Dufo[ur], who has bitter personal reasons for taking vengeance on the English. He offers safe passes for the whole party—on condition that Mary remains behind as his wife. With internment as the alternative, what choice has she?

Yet cold, sarcastic and disfigured as he is she finds herself drawn to the enigmatic Captain. If her situation really is so terrible why does she fail to take advantage of the opportunities to escape?

'. . . that sweet enemy, France.'

Sir Philip Sidney

That Sweet Enemy
Marjorie May

MILLS & BOON LIMITED
London · Sydney · Toronto

First published in Great Britain 1982 by
Mills & Boon Limited, 15–16 Brook's Mews,
London W1A 1DR

ISBN 0 263 73785 3

Set in 10 on 11 pt Times

Photoset by Rowland Phototypesetting Ltd
Bury St Edmunds, Suffolk
Made and printed in Great Britain by
Cox & Wyman Ltd, Reading

To my friends in Waltham Abbey

AUTHOR'S NOTE

The term 'internment' for the detention of enemy non-combatants in wartime did not come into use until circa 1870, but it has been used here for convenience.

CHAPTER
ONE

THE large berline and the smaller travelling-coach climbed the road out of Lausanne at a good pace, for the horses were fresh after their two-day rest, and the broad pastures of the Freiburge, bright with the flowers of early summer, soon opened out on either side, with a pleasant view of the Jura beyond.

Mary Burns stared out of the window of the berline, her dreamy brown eyes only half aware of the passing scenery, and worried about the immediate future. So far all had gone well, but there were still at least five towns through which they must pass before they entered Baden, and it had been impossible to discover whether the French or the Swiss were in control of any or all of them.

'So fair a prospect must rejoice the heart!' declaimed Mr Brown in one of his few perfect iambic pentameters. 'Do you not agree, Miss Burns?'

Mary forced herself out of her preoccupation to give him a polite smile and a murmured 'Oh, indeed!' He was a handsome young man, in an ethereal fashion, with fair hair and grey eyes, and an interesting air of delicacy, for he had suffered a severe congestion of the lungs in childhood, which was why he had spent the previous winter in the small village of Cannes on the warm Mediterranean coast.

'It'd rejoice my heart a damn—dashed sight more if it wasn't likely to be swarming with Frenchies!' remarked Sir John Robbins, the owner of berline, coach and horses, and the employer of the two drivers, William and Henry. His good-humoured red face had taken on a distinctly anxious look these past few days, ever since he had found a letter from England awaiting him in Grenoble, containing the news that the Peace of Amiens had broken down and the war between Britain and France was about to be renewed. This information had been confirmed by the Governor of Genève when they paid him a courtesy call on arrival in his city, and he had kindly added the warning that a state of war had, in fact, existed since 17th May, nine days before, and that the First Consul was said to have ordered the arrest and internment of all British subjects who had the misfortune to find themselves in French territory.

'As you are here,' he had pointed out. 'However, the courier bringing me instructions in the matter will not arrive until tomorrow morning, by which time, no doubt, you will have crossed the border into Vaud, which is, of course, a Free Canton and not part of the Helvetic Confederation.'

'Does that—er—make a difference?' enquired Sir John, who found the new political arrangements of Europe most confusingly unlike those of his previous visits to the Continent in the far-off days before the French Revolution.

'But of course!' the Governor had replied with a Gallic expressiveness of hands and eyebrows. 'The Helvetic Confederation is under the protection of the First Consul! I should advise you to enter Vaud and remain there!'

As a result of this conversation, Sir John and Lady Sarah, his wife, Mary and Mr Brown, together with Lady Sarah's maid, the gentlemen's valets and the two coachmen, had hastened to leave Genève very early the next morning, hardly daring to draw breath until they were safely past the customs post at Versoix, where the official had kept them waiting an agonising fifteen minutes while he carefully spelled out every word on their passports, and then counted all their trunks and boxes three times over, apparently arriving at a different total each time.

The greatest strain of that quarter-hour had fallen on Mary, for she was the only one of the party who spoke French, Sir John and Lady Sarah having forgotten all but a few polite phrases, and Mr Brown disclaiming all knowledge of the language. Eventually, as they seemed likely to remain forever at Versoix, Mary had uttered the words which had so far acted with magical effect on every French official they had met since they left Paris the previous summer:

'As you may see, our papers have been signed by General Mortier.'

'Indeed!' replied the official. 'All is in order. A pleasant journey to you, and a swift return to our beautiful France!' and he actually handed Mary back into the berline.

'Thank you! Oh, I hope so!' she had replied fervently, sinking back into her seat with a sigh of relief as the berline rolled across the border into Vaud and safety.

The trouble was, however, that they could not possibly consider remaining in Vaud until the war ended, but must go on through the Helvetic Confederation to Bâle, and hope then to cross the Rhine into Baden, whence they could make a safe journey through the German States to Hamburg and thence home. Lady Sarah had insisted on a couple of days' rest in Lausanne, for she was weary of travelling, and Sir John had reluctantly agreed.

'I wish we'd never left home!' he had grumbled. 'If I'd had the least idea that we'd land in such a pickle, I'd never have agreed to wintering in the south of France!'

'Well, there was no way of knowing that this Bonaparte creature would prove so perfidious and uncivilised!' Lady Sarah had pointed out. 'With the Peace of Amiens being signed, it seemed such a good opportunity to escape the winter at home, for you know how it always makes me ill, and to show Mary a little of Abroad and give an opportunity to meet some interesting people. Heaven knows, life at home in Broadwood is dull enough for older and settled folk like ourselves, and it's dreadfully so for a girl of no more than twenty, like dear Mary!'

Thinking back over the past year as the berline rolled across the Freiburge towards Moudon, Mary was not sure whether it had been worth the present anxieties. Of course, it had been exciting to travel after spending almost the whole of her twenty years of life in a small, isolated village, where the future held no prospect but a gentle decline into old-maidery. She had seen Paris, and actually met the First Consul, who had been a disappointment, being no taller than herself, with lank hair which looked suspiciously thin about the temples, a disagreeable expression and a marked lack of charm.

On the other hand, Mr Brown was very charming. He had appeared in Cannes not long after their own arrival there, and had made himself agreeable to Lady Sarah, and particularly to Mary. He was very eligible, being connected through his father to a Marquess and through his mother to a Duke, and his sister was married to an Earl. Mary thought none the worse of him for that, for he was not the least high in the instep or condescending in his manner to lesser mortals, and she had found much pleasure in his company, eventually even toying in her imagination with the idea of abandoning her life-long predilection for heroes of the tall, dark variety and considering the possibility of attraction in a man of fair complexion and medium height.

There was, of course, the added interest of his delicate health. If Mary had a fault, it was an over-active and romantic imagination, fostered by a dull life with too little to occupy her mind, and she had dwelt happily on the picture of herself tending a tidily and not-too-ill hero, and receiving the grateful smile which would appear on the wan but handsome face, marked but not marred by patient suffering, at the magical touch of her fair hand on a fevered brow.

To add still more to his attractions, Mr Brown was a poet. Admittedly, his verses were woefully lame, and she had found herself inclined to shake him on the occasion, soon after they left Cannes, when a wheel of the berline broke, and he had draped himself gracefully against the nearest tree to discourse lyrically on the beauties of nature instead of doing something useful, especially when one of the beauties of nature had stung her painfully on the neck. On the other hand, he had shown a marked interest in her, even to the extent of proposing, with becoming hesitation and many parenthetical apologies for his temerity, that he might accompany the Robbins and Mary on their journey home. He spoke fluent German, and as this would facilitate Sir John's wish to travel by way of the Swiss cantons and the German States, his offer was graciously accepted.

By now, Mary was aware that Mr Brown's interest in her was considerable, and she was almost certain that before long he would be making a more personal proposal. He had mentioned two or three times that he hoped to introduce her to his family, and surely that could only mean that he meant to make an Offer. If he did, she would be foolish to decline it when there was no other prospect of marriage in view and precious little chance of anything better appearing in the future! After all, most young ladies who married did so because an eligible man had Offered, not because they were swept off their feet by the tempestuous storms of Love, and she had no particular fault to find with Mr Brown.

Her thoughts wandered back to the previous day,

when he had kindly offered to escort her on her explor-
ation of Lausanne, and he had been most attentive.
Mary had welcomed his presence, for he was a pleasant
companion, but she had felt a little shy of being alone
with him, for she was doubtful about the precise nature
of her feelings towards him, so she had kept to the
well-frequented places and avoided diversions into side-
chapels in the cathedral or deserted streets outside it.
Consequently, Mr Brown's only chance to say anything
particularly private to her had occurred when they were
standing on the cathedral terrace admiring the view, and
there happened for a moment to be no-one else near
enough to hear.

'I say, Miss Burns!' he had said, after a quick glance
around them. 'I shall be excessively sorry when our
travels come to an end, save for one thing!'

'Indeed,' Mary had replied. 'I fear we still have a long
way to go, and may yet encounter serious difficulties to
delay us! I shall not be at all sorry to reach home safely,
and I protest that I'm really quite shaken to pieces with
the rough roads we have traversed!'

'But even the roughest roads are endurable in such
pleasant company!'

Mary had given him a non-committal smile, wondering if he would consider internment endurable in her
company if Fate and the First Consul so decreed, which
Heaven forbid!

'I wonder what those particularly sharp mountains
over there are called,' she had remarked.

'Do you not wonder what is the one thing which
tempers my regrets?' Mr Brown had sounded a trifle
piqued.

'If you wish to tell me.'

'It's the thought that I shall have the pleasure of
making you known to my family, and thereafter learning
to know you better myself!' he had announced, with the

air of a conjuror producing a particularly admirable rabbit from a round hat and two handkerchiefs.

Mary had given him a vague smile, surprised at the distinct feeling of apprehension which his words had aroused in her, from which she could only conclude that she was not altogether happy at the prospect of being known better by Mr Brown. In fact, if he had meant what she thought he did, she had to admit that the idea of marrying him was not as pleasant as she had once thought it might be.

'You are very quiet, Mary,' Lady Sarah's gentle voice broke into her thoughts. 'You're not still worrying about the French, surely? I was assured in Lausanne that they have no garrisons in Vaud.'

'No, but we have to leave Vaud and travel through territory where they may have garrisons to reach Bâle,' Mary blurted out, and then wished she had at least phrased her sentence more carefully, for she had no wish to alarm her friend.

'I'm sure we have no need to feel apprehension,' Lady Sarah replied comfortably. 'If we do happen to meet with a few French officials, your command of the language has enabled you to deal with their kind most effectively in the past, and we have Mr Brown to protect us!'

Mary managed a smile, but thought to herself that Mr Brown was likely to prove too delicate in health and sensibilities to deal effectively with the rough, ungentlemanly fellows who nowadays formed the officialdom of the French Republic. If anyone was called upon to protect the party, it was more likely to be herself!

'General Mortier's name on our papers is our best guarantee,' put in Sir John. 'What a stroke of luck that he happened to sign them before we left Paris! He seems to command more respect among his countrymen than even Bonaparte! One reference to that signature has been sufficient to solve every problem so far, and I've no doubt it will do so again!'

He sounded as bluffly confident as ever, but Mary wondered if he really thought that the General's name would save them from internment if the First Consul had decreed otherwise. Perhaps, if the worst happened, she might mention that they were acquainted with General Bonaparte—after all, they had actually met him, however fleetingly!

After the anxieties of the morning, their passage through Moudon was an anti-climax, for they were not even stopped to show their papers, nor at Payerne, where they stayed the night, and in neither town were any French officials or soldiers to be seen. The travellers exchanged a few remarks of relief, and began to think that perhaps they had worried unnecessarily.

The drive from Payerne to Berne next day was similarly uneventful, and enlivened only by the beauty of the valley around Avenches, with its terraced vineyards, and the quaint appearance of the little walled town. They reached Berne in the afternoon, and were stopped at the gate by a solitary Swiss official, who collected their passports and enquired which inn they meant to patronise. Mary asked his advice, and he directed them to a very picturesque and comfortable place in the Marktgasse, where their papers were returned to them as they sat at supper.

'Could someone perhaps inform me,' Mr Brown enquired earnestly, 'but is Berne not a part of the Helvetic Confederation? My geographical knowledge is not of the best, I fear.'

'Certainly it is,' replied Sir John confidently, and then, less confidently, 'At least, I think so. Things have been somewhat complicated in this part of the world in recent years!'

'I've seen no sign of any French soldiers or officials

since we crossed the border out of France yesterday,' Mr Brown continued. 'Do you think it possible that you may have misunderstood the Governor of Genève? I hesitate to make this suggestion, of course, but one understands that a—er—slightly unfamiliar language may disguise shades of meaning, and saying that the Confederation is under the protection of the First Consul may not actually imply that his edicts have any application here . . .'

Mary was amused by his delicate way of hinting that her French comprehension was not of the first order, but she was firmly convinced that she had not misunderstood the Governor, and said so.

'The only thing that I'm not sure about is exactly what he meant by saying that English travellers were to be arrested and interned,' she added. 'I assume that he meant that they are to be prisoners of war, but I've never heard of such a thing before.'

'Mm,' agreed Sir John. 'That seemed to be his meaning, but I've not heard of such a thing before either. It sounds positively barbarous, but that's the new France!' and he sighed.

Mr Brown, however, remained sceptical about any threat to their freedom existing in the Helvetic Confederation, and the others began to think that he might well be right. They looked about the city in the morning, visiting the Cathedral and the Market, and seeing no sign whatever of any French presence, and very little of any Swiss officials either. They left Berne without hindrance after an early luncheon, having only twenty miles or so to go on a good road to Soleure, which they reached in the afternoon.

It was a walled city, with gates guarded by very stumpy, fat towers, and an Italianate collection of domes and spires clustered above the cathedral rising over a huddle of dark-red tiled roofs. From a distance, Mary thought it looked charming, and quite a suitable setting

for a fairy-tale, and she was so busy admiring the picture
it presented that it was a rude shock to find one detail of
it suddenly and unexpectedly appearing at the carriage-
door—a French corporal, who bade them step down and
present their passports.

Since Mary usually dealt with such matters, she had
taken to carrying all nine sets of papers in her capacious
travelling-reticule, and, for the first time, this proved a
disadvantage. The corporal in charge required her to
point out to which individual each set of papers be-
longed, and he also wished to establish which of the
gentry employed each of the servants. He seemed puzzled that Mary had no maid of her own, and that she and
Mr Brown were not related to one another or to the
Robbins. Eventually, however, he straightened all the
papers into a neat bundle and tied them with a piece of
string which an ordinary soldier quickly placed in the
hand which he held out for it.

'You may proceed to the inn which this man will show
you,' he said, indicating one of his soldiers.

'Is it a good inn?' Mary enquired.

'It is the inn where you will stay until Captain Dufour
decides what to do with you,' was the ominous reply.

Mary joined the others, who had returned to the
berline, and passed this on.

'And who is Captain Dufour?' demanded Sir John. 'I
don't care for the sound of this!'

Their guide mounted the box beside William, and the
two carriages rumbled through the gates into the town,
then across the bridge to the older section, north of the
river, winding slowly through busy, narrow streets between tall, shuttered houses and across squares enlivened by fountains. There were many French soldiers
in the streets, both infantry and cavalry, and the travellers exchanged apprehensive glances.

The inn was a large, rambling building with gables and

chimneypots sprouting from its tiled roof. Their guide
directed them through an archway, which seemed to be
the only entrance, into a yard with stables and a coach-
house along two sides, and shuttered windows on the
other two, with another row of windows above. Mary
looked round at the blank windows and felt trapped,
shut in. Her sensation of helplessness increased when
two more soldiers closed the leaves of a wooden gate
with iron spikes on the top across the entrance.

A cheerful, red-cheeked man in shirt and breeches,
topped by a large white apron, came out of the inn to
greet them.

'I'm Johann,' he announced in French with a strong
German accent. 'Anything you want, call for Johann!'
He ushered them inside, sent a couple of menservants to
unload their bags, and ostlers for the horses, punctu-
ating his order with odd words of welcome in various
languages, eventually returning to French to explain the
situation.

It appeared that the inn had been commandeered by
the French to serve as a headquarters for the officer in
charge of civilian movement in this part of the Helvetic
Republic. He occupied one wing, with his men, and the
other was used for travellers who, for one reason or
another, could not be allowed to continue their jour-
neys.

'They mostly stay one or two nights, while the Captain
sorts things out. Sometimes they have the wrong papers,
or the wrong signatures, or maybe none at all,' Johann
explained. 'The Captain is very efficient, and puts them
straight as quick as he can, and then they can go on their
way, or back where they came from, or . . . or . . .
whatever . . .'

The inconclusive conclusion of this speech made Mary
give Johann a very sharp look. 'What do you mean by
"whatever"?' she asked.

'Well, there were three Englishmen a few days ago
. . . young gentlemen. He sent them somewhere with an
escort . . . into France, I believe . . .'

'We're English,' Mary said nervously.

'Er . . . yes . . . well, I don't wish to alarm you . . .
They were young, healthy gentlemen, of military age,
you understand . . .'

'Yes, of course,' Mary replied with more confidence
than she felt. 'Where may we find this Captain . . . ?'

'Dufour. He'll send for you, Madame, when he's
ready. Meanwhile, would you care to order supper?'

Mary consulted with Sir John, and supper was ordered, then a neat chambermaid showed them to their
rooms, which were clean, but not very large, and overlooked the courtyard. Sir John asked for something
larger, looking on the street, and was told, with many
apologies, that the rooms looking on the street were
kept locked, but a slightly larger room was found for
him.

Supper was served in a small breakfast-parlour, for
which Johann apologised, explaining that there were
two proper dining-rooms, but they were being used by
the French soldiers. The English group perforce shared
the room with a German family from Bavaria and three
Swiss merchants, who were very indignant about their
enforced stay and muttered among themselves in German all the time. Mr Brown said that they were com-
plaining about having to satisfy French soldiers about
their right to travel in their own country, and describing
the First Consul in terms which Mr Brown would not
care to apply to anyone, however tyrannical and mis-
guided, but added that he had every sympathy for them
otherwise, a sentiment to which the others subscribed,
and showed it by smiling in friendly fashion at the ag-
grieved Swiss, who nodded back in a suspicious manner.

Mr Brown also conversed with the Bavarians, and

learned from them that Soleure, having for centuries been the residence of the French ambassador to the Cantons, had now become virtually the main garrison town of the French Army in the Republic. Mr Brown enquired why there was a French Army in the country at all, if it was supposed to be an independent republic, and the Bavarian gentleman replied that the First Consul thought it necessary to protect the new constitution which he had recently devised for the long-suffering Swiss.

'There are about 800 French soldiers in the town,' Mr Brown relayed to the others, 'and our friends here think we were quite mad to enter this town at all! They say we should have gone straight to Bâle. We could have cross-ed the Aare at Wangen, where there are no French at all, and they say it is quite easy to slip across the frontier at Bâle!'

'Why are they here, then?' asked Sir John, sounding irritable. He was worried about their situation, and re-sented Mr Brown's tone, which seemed to imply that it was Sir John's fault that they had come to Soleure.

Mr Brown embarked on further German conversa-tion, and presently explained that the Bavarians had both family and business connections in the town, and were leaving in the morning, having received their passes from Captain Dufour just before supper. He was, they said, a very cold man. As soon as they had finished their meal, they hurried away to their rooms, pausing only for the mother to make a voluble speech to Lady Sarah, who understood not a word, and the father to shake hands with Sir John and Mr Brown, wagging his head and pursing his lips as if he feared the worst for them. He made a stiff, heel-clicking bow to the ladies, while his two little girls dropped neat curtseys.

Mr Brown enquired of Johann, who spoke German as well as French, if there was a sitting-room available, but the innkeeper explained, with many expressions of regret, that the only sitting-room was in the possession of the French, and there was really nowhere for guests but this small parlour. The travellers perforce remained where they were, and, once the tables had been cleared, made themselves as comfortable as they could near the window, while the Swiss men sat round a small table in the far corner, heads together and muttering crossly among themselves.

By nine o'clock, Sir John had grown very restive, and several times went to the door to put his head out and glare about the square hall outside—a pointless exercise, as there was no-one about to see him, but at least it gave him the feeling that he was doing something.

Lady Sarah produced a piece of embroidery and put in a few stitches, drawing the candles near her so that she could see, and thereby condemning Mary to outer twilight as she was sitting on the opposite side of the table. She had a book in her reticule, but could not see to read it without depriving Lady Sarah of the light. Mr Brown produced some paper and a pencil from his pocket and began to write a poem, leaning as close to the candles as Lady Sarah's embroidery-bag would allow. At least, Mary judged that this was what he was doing, going by the long pauses for thought and the weighty sighs which punctuated the activity.

'Who the devil does this Captain Dufour think he is?' Sir John muttered irritably, prowling about the room. 'If he doesn't put in an appearance in the next quarter-hour, I shall go to bed, and he may go hang!'

About twenty minutes later, there was a peremptory knock at the door, followed by the entrance of a French soldier, who stated briefly that the English must come to the Captain. Sir John was clearly about to take exception to this, but Mary forestalled him by translating the message in politer terms, including some mention of 'please' and 'if you would be so good' and added on her own account that the sooner the interview was over, the sooner they might all retire.

The door from the courtyard to the interior of the inn was set about half-way along the left-hand side as one stood with one's back to the street. It opened into a square hall, with a tiled stove on one side and a staircase leading to the upper floor on the other. The supper-room door was near the foot of the stairs, with a cur-tained arch nearby which appeared to lead to the domestic quarters in the front of the building. Another arch on the opposite side led towards the back, and it was through this that the soldier led them, passing an open door, through which Mary caught a glimpse of a large room in which half a dozen soldiers were sitting about at their ease, reading or playing cards.

They then traversed a short passage and rounded a corner into a longer one, which had windows on to the courtyard on the right, and two or three doors on the left. The soldier rapped on the first door, then opened it and stood back, gesturing to the four English people to go in.

It was quite a large room, with a scrubbed board floor brightened by a few scattered rugs. A large open fire-place with neatly-stacked logs set ready for use occupied much of the wall to the right, and a big wooden dresser full of plates and dishes, apparently more for decoration than for use, faced it from the opposite wall. There were five or six plain wooden chairs standing about, larger high-backed wooden armchairs with patchwork cush-ions on either side of the hearth, and a sofa made of dark, heavy-looking wood, covered with crimson velvet stood diagonally to the left of the centre of the room, half-facing the most dominant feature, a large flat-topped desk, supporting an inkstand, several neat stacks of paper, and a four-branched candelabrum.

These candles provided the only source of light in the room, which was consequently gloomy and full of shadows, for even the three long windows facing the door from behind the desk were covered with dark velvet curtains. It struck Mary that the room was not unlike a stage-set, with that single pool of light concentrating the attention of the audience on the desk and the occupant of the chair behind it.

But the chair was empty. The room was occupied by William and Henry, the coachmen, and the other servants, who were standing in a little huddle between the door and the fireplace. As the gentry entered, their faces turned towards the door, looking white and frightened, and Sir John at once enquired if they were comfortably lodged and had been well-fed. William, as spokesman, assured his master that they were well-content, and Sir John nodded affably, saying 'Good, good. Now, we'll get all this business sorted out as soon as this Captain What'shisname appears, and I expect we'll be on our way in the morning.'

The servants greeted this with murmurs and uncertain smiles, and Lady Sarah, after a swift assessment of the various chairs available, advanced to the sofa and gracefully seated herself. Mary was about to join her when a slight movement in the shadows beyond the desk caught her attention.

At first, she thought that one of the curtains moved, but then she realised that a darker shadow stood against it, and she had just arrived at the realisation that someone was standing with his back to the room, apparently looking out through a narrow opening in the curtains, when the figure turned and moved forward into the light.

He was tall, and dressed in the dark blue uniform of a French officer, relieved only by a little white lacing and silver buttons, and his hair was very dark. As he moved, he appeared to give an odd lurch, and then he hooked a

walking-stick on to the edge of the desk, and Mary
realised that he was lame. The light fell on his face, and
she saw that his left eye was covered by a black patch,
only partly hiding two ugly red scars which seamed his
cheek and ran up into his hair, which was brushed forward over his brow in the style known as 'à la Titus'. His
other eye was deep-set and black, and briefly glanced
over the others before fixing on Mary.

'I believe you understand French,' he said in that
language. 'Be so kind as to sit there,' indicating a chair
placed squarely in front of the desk, 'and I shall address
myself to you, so that you may translate what I say to
your companions.'

Mary obediently stepped forward to the chair and sat
down on it, folding her hands on her reticule in her lap,
and setting her black-slippered feet neatly side-by-side.
She was not aware that, in her plain muslin dress and
white shawl, her brown ringlets caught up in a simple
chignon, she looked very young and vulnerable. She
fixed her large brown eyes on the Captain's face and
essayed a nervous smile.

'Pray ask your friends to seat themselves,' the Captain
said. Mary did so, and he waited until Mr Brown and Sir
John had found chairs, the latter signalling to the servants to sit as well, which they did rather gingerly, not
being used to sitting in the presence of the gentry. When
everyone was settled, there was a moment's silence,
while Captain Dufour sat down in his chair and stared
across the desk at Mary.

CHAPTER
TWO

HE was now near enough to the candles for Mary to see his face more clearly, and she found little cause for comfort there. Considering his dark hair, and the fact that the weather had been warm and sunny for some time, she would have expected him to be somewhat swarthy, but he was pale, the scar providing the only notable colour in his face, which was lean, with grooves cut from the strong nose to the firm, thin-lipped mouth. His one visible eye appeared black and unfathomable, and fixed unwaveringly on her face.

'Ask him why he's kept us waiting such a damn' long time!' Sir John grunted irascibly.

'We were beginning to think we should not have the opportunity to make your acquaintance tonight,' Mary translated.

The eye flicked momentarily towards Sir John, and then back to Mary, and the level black brows rose a fraction.

'My apologies for the delay. I received your papers only half an hour ago, when I returned here. I have been at the Commandant's residence for some hours.' His voice was cold and dry, and as devoid of expression as that eye, which was beginning to intimidate Mary. On the other hand, he was well-spoken, and clearly a gentleman, which was a pleasant surprise after some of the officials they had encountered in France.

He turned away to pick up one of the piles of papers on his desk, which he placed before him, then selected the topmost one and read it. Mary craned her neck a little, and saw that these were their passports.

'The two men in livery are presumably the coachmen,' Captain Dufour said, laying aside the first and second sets of papers. 'The other two men will be the valets of Sir John Robbins, and Mr Roger Brown. The woman is the maid of Lady Sarah Robbins. Why have you no maid?'

The eye was back on Mary's face at that, and she found herself answering defensively, 'I had only a cook-maid and two serving-men at home. Ellen said she would be happy to look after my things as well as Lady Sarah's, to save me having to find someone.'

'*Obsidian*,' she thought. '*That eye is like obsidian— glassy, opaque, saying nothing! I don't know what he's thinking! His face doesn't give the slightest hint, nor his eye . . .*' She felt completely at a loss, only now realising how much, in her dealings with other people, she depended on what she could read in their expressions, and particularly in their eyes. This man's face was a closed book, a sardonic mask.

Captain Dufour looked down at the passports again, and spread the remaining four packets in a fan before him.

'John Robbins, Baronet, Sarah, his wife, Miss Marie Burns, Mr Roger Brown.' He pronounced the names fairly correctly, although with a French accent, apart from the 'Marie'.

'Mary,' she corrected automatically.

In reply, she received a very cold and piercing look, and an expressionless repetition of 'Marie,' and she shivered.

'Why are you four persons travelling together through the Helvetic Republic?'

'Sir John and Lady Sarah wished to spend the past winter in Cannes, and they invited me to accompany them. We made the acquaintance of Mr Brown there, and he decided to travel with us on the way home.'

Captain Dufour remained silent, and Mary thought she had never seen anyone sit so still. He did not appear to move a muscle, and might have been carved out of granite. She shivered again.

'You should wear a warmer shawl in the evening,' he observed dispassionately. 'We are more than 400 metres above sea-level here. Why do you return home this way?'

'We wish to travel through the German states.'

'You are aware that England and France are at war?'

'Yes, but Switzerland is neutral . . .'

'On the contrary. The Helvetic Republic is under the protection of France.'

His tone seemed to Mary particularly dry, almost sarcastic, in his second sentence, but there was still no flicker of expression.

'Will that . . . affect us?' she asked hesitantly.

'My orders are to detain British subjects for internment at my discretion.'

As he did not enlarge on this, Mary waited a moment, and then prompted, 'At your discretion?'

'That simply means that I am not to plague Paris with questions concerning individual cases. If a person is clearly incapable of harming French interests in any way, I may allow him to pass—otherwise, not. If this were France, there would be no choice, you understand?'

'I'm sure none of us is capable of harming France,' Mary began with an assumption of confidence, but he cut in before she could continue.

'Come now! Six men, all quite well able to shoulder a musket? Three women far short of their dotage?'

'But Sir John is past fifty, and Mr Brown's health is poor! Neither would ever consider joining the army! The others are servants, and couldn't be spared, even if they had any desire to enlist!'

'You English are fortunate that you have any choice in the matter!' was the curt rejoinder to that.

'And what could Lady Sarah, or Ellen, or I do to harm France? Surely the French don't make war on women?'

Surprisingly, this seemed to cut through his mask, for he scowled and said brusquely, 'Why not, when women make war on Frenchmen?' in a remarkably bitter tone.

There was silence for a moment, and then Mary ventured cautiously, 'Perhaps you would be kind enough to arrange for us to see the Commandant . . . ?'

'General Eppler is not concerned in this matter. My office is a separate function, not under his control.'

'Then . . . to whom are you responsible?'

'To Paris.'

Mary felt that the time had come to play one of her trumps.

'We are acquainted with General Mortier,' she said firmly. 'No doubt he will vouch for us. He signed our passports when we were in Paris, as you may see.'

'Naturally—he was Governor of the city when you were there,' was the unimpressed reply. 'Unfortunately, he is no longer in Paris, but presently engaged in the invasion of Hanover.'

Mary realised that this man was very different from the semi-educated and not over-bright officials she had encountered in the past. His accent, mode of speech and appearance placed him firmly in the ranks of the gentry, and he was shrewd and intelligent as well. His rather curt manner was probably due to the fact that he was dealing with the enemies of his country. It was not with any real expectation of success that she played her second trump.

'We are also acquainted with the First Consul!' she said briskly.

'My commiserations!' was the unexpected reply, still in that dry, expressionless voice.

Mary stared at him wide-eyed, and found the eye as

unenlightening as ever, but a muscle twitched slightly by the firm mouth, and she thought he might possibly be amused. Well, now—there *was* some sort of emotion concealed behind the iron mask, then! Bitterness, and now, possibly, humour!

'Do you wish me to write to General Bonaparte, to request special passes for you?' the cold voice enquired. 'It was he who ordered internment, you realise.'

'No. I don't suppose he'd remember us,' Mary admitted dejectedly.

'I do wish, m'dear, that you'd tell us something of what the fellow is saying!' Sir John interjected, quite mildly, under the circumstances.

'Excuse me,' said Mary to Captain Dufour, who made a slight, elegant bow without actually moving anything but his head. 'It's very difficult,' she continued in English, half-turning towards the others. 'He says he has orders to intern anyone who might possibly be able to harm French interests, and he considers that we all fall into that category! I'm trying to convince him otherwise, but I don't think he appreciates how very unlikely it is that any one of the men here would ever join the army . . .'

'Have you mentioned our friend, the General?' asked Sir John. Mr Brown was busy expressing disgust at the mere idea of the army, and the servants looked anxious and bewildered.

'Yes, but he's not in the least impressed! I mentioned the First Consul as well, but he—he seemed to find that amusing!'

Sir John scratched his nose reflectively. 'D'you think we could offer him a good, big, er . . . ?'

'Bribe?' completed Mary in hushed tones. 'I think not—he's not in that class of persons at all . . .'

'I should not advise you to try!' Captain Dufour's incisive voice cut in, speaking English.

Mary swung back to face him.

'Oh! You understand English!' she cried accusingly.

He regarded her silently for a moment, and then replied calmly, 'If necessary. We will continue in French.'

'But if we speak English, the others will understand!'

He let out his breath in something like a sigh, and then said 'I do not care to use your language. It holds many . . . unpleasant memories, which would prejudice me against you. We will continue in French.'

His tone admitted of no questions, and brooked no argument, so Mary perforce asked in French, 'If . . . if we are to be interned, where will you send us?'

'To France. The men to the fortress at Sedan. I have not yet been informed where female prisoners are to be kept, but it will probably be Besançon or Auxonne.'

'We'd be separated?' Mary was horrified. 'Oh, but that's cruel! Poor Lady Sarah . . . she couldn't bear to be parted from Sir John!'

This had no visible effect, but he said quietly, 'I've not come to any decision yet. You will remain here, in the inn, while I consider what shall be done with you.'

'How long do you think . . . ?'

As she tailed off nervously, he waited a moment, then one eyebrow quirked a fraction, and he enquired, 'The war will last? I've no idea.'

'Naturally. I meant, how long will it take you to decide?'

He sketched the faintest suggestion of a Gallic shrug and replied, 'A few days—a week, perhaps. Maybe more. I'm sure you would not wish me to make a hurried decision? I have to judge the likelihood that your servants may wish to fight for their country, or that Sir John or Mr Brown may be seduced by the attractions of a military or naval life. There is also the question of Mr Brown's health.'

'There is no call for sarcasm!' Mary's indignation gave
her a sudden flare-up of courage. 'You know very well
that no servant in a good place and his right mind would
enlist in the British Army! Sir John is a country land-
owner, and knows nothing of military affairs, and Mr
Brown is a poet!'

'So was Bertrand du Guesclin,' Captain Dufour replied calmly, the muscle by his mouth twitching again.
'And your own Sir Philip Sidney, for that matter! The
servants may not consider themselves in a good place. I
shall observe you all for a time, and ask a few questions,
and make a decision based on what I discover. You are
free to move about in your own part of the inn, where
Johann will provide for your reasonable needs. You will,
of course, be the guests of the French government.'

'May we not go out into the town?' Mary asked.

'If there is anything which Johann cannot provide, you
may apply to Sergeant Girard.'

Mary assumed from this that they might not go out
into the town. As the Captain did not appear to have
anything more to say, she turned to the others and told
them most of what he had said, omitting the information
that, if they were to be interned, the men would be
separated from the women, for she did not wish to
distress Lady Sarah or Ellen until—and unless—it
became necessary.

When she had finished, there was a few moments'
silence while her audience grappled with what they had
just heard, and then Sir John rose to his feet and said
firmly, 'Well, we're all fagged with travel and worry, so
we'd best retire and try to sleep on the problem. We'll
talk about it in the morning. Goodnight to you, Captain,'
and he gave a hand to his wife and led her from the room.

Captain Dufour stood up and gave a slight bow as
everyone else began to move towards the door. Everyone, that is, except Mary. She rose and took a few steps,

and then turned back, her lips parting as if she was about
to speak, her brown eyes very large and anxious. The
Captain had moved back a little from his desk and was
now a dark shadow against the curtains again, lit only by
the faint gleam of candlelight on his silver buttons and
the pale blur of his face.

'Yes, Miss Burns?' he enquired.

Mary hesitated, not sure what she had meant to say,
wondering fleetingly if it would be any use to make an
appeal for mercy, then decided that it would probably be
useless.

'Nothing. Goodnight, Captain,' she said.

'Goodnight, Miss Burns. Sleep well,' he replied, his
voice perhaps a fraction less cold.

She could only suppose that his reply was his idea of
humour, and she swept towards the door, head erect,
feeling helplessly angry. Mr Brown was still standing in
the doorway, apparently waiting for her, but this was
not, it seemed, his only reason, for he said in agitated
tones, 'I say, Miss Burns! Would you be so kind as to ask
the Captain if we may summon a doctor?'

'Is he ill?' the Captain enquired in French.

'He says, are you ill?' Mary passed on.

'Not yet, but I've a slightly sore throat, and I feel sure I
have taken cold,' Mr Brown replied earnestly. 'I hope I
may not, but I very much fear that all the signs indicate
the worst!'

Once more, Mary turned back towards the Captain,
suppressing a strong desire to indulge in hysterics, and
once more the Captain replied to the question before she
could translate it.

'Tell the poor fellow that he shall have a doctor if he
needs one.' There was not even a hint of impatience in
the dispassionate voice.

'Thank you. Goodnight,' and Mary firmly closed the
door behind her.

Of course, none of them slept well, and it was barely eight o'clock the next morning when they were gathered in the small parlour for breakfast. The Bavarian family had already left, and the Swiss gentlemen's demeanour changed abruptly halfway through their croissants and coffee, when a burly sergeant brought them their passes and told them they might leave when they chose.

'I only pray that he may soon say the same to us!' Lady Sarah murmured to Mary, who was making a determined effort to eat a croissant spread with cherry conserve, but finding it difficult to force down.

'I'm sure it will not be long,' she replied. 'We have only to convince the Captain that we're harmless.'

'Harmless!' snorted Sir John, who had angrily munched his way through four croissants already. 'I don't feel harmless, I may tell you! I'd like to take the fellow's stick and push it down his throat, and close his other eye with my fist!'

'He seems a very unfeeling person,' Mr Brown croaked morosely, and took another sip of the honey and lemon concoction with which he was cossetting his sore throat. He was now showing every sign of the onset of a heavy cold. 'Not a smile or a kind word for anyone, no sympathy for our predicament, not even a polite enquiry as to how we do this morning! Most unfeeling— a veritable icicle—positively adamantine!' It was a pity that the effect of this hyperbole was spoiled by his cold turning the last word into 'adabantide'.

'What are we to do?' Mary asked quietly, pushing her plate away and pouring herself some more coffee.

'I thig I shall go bag to bed,' Mr Brown said despondently. 'I dode feel ad all de thig.'

'Perhaps you should, then,' Lady Sarah said in a gentle, sympathetic voice, as no-one else answered him.

'I don't see what we can do!' Sir John said, absently reaching for another croissant. 'I don't know anything about this General Eppler, except that Johann tells me he commands the garrison, but Captain Dufour and his merry men ain't part of the garrison, and don't come under his orders, so I don't see much use in appealing to him. Don't we know anyone important in France? We must have visited Paris half a dozen times in the old days—surely we know someone with some influence?'

'We knew a great many important people, but that was before the Revolution and the War—I fear none of them would be important now—most of them are not even alive!' Lady Sarah said sadly. 'Perhaps if Mary and I went to the Captain and pleaded . . .'

'I'm damned if I'll plead to a damned Frog, nor let my womenfolk be reduced to so much as *asking* him for anything! Sorry, m'dear.' The apology was for his infelicitous language, not his rejection of his wife's suggestion.

As no-one else had a suggestion to offer, they sat in silence, thinking. Mr Brown sipped his soothing draught and sniffed unhappily at intervals, Lady Sarah toyed with a piece of bread, Mary drank her coffee, and Sir John ate another croissant, and then there was a brisk knock at the door, and the burly sergeant entered. He had a round, red face and matching nose, and grizzled, close-cropped hair, and, unlike the rather shapeless, wrinkled garments worn by most of the French infantrymen Mary had seen, his uniform fitted him and was clean and well-pressed.

'Mam'selle Bournz?' he enquired, looking at Mary.

'Yes?'

'Sergeant Girard, at your service. Captain Dufour presents his compliments, and wishes to know if the younger gentleman requires a doctor.'

'Do you require a doctor, Mr Brown?' Mary relayed.

He replied fervently, 'Oh, indeed I do! I hab such a code! I hope id bay nod be *la grippe*!'

'Yes, if you please,' Mary passed back to the Sergeant, who came to attention in acknowledgment, then stood himself at ease and continued, 'And Captain Dufour requests that you will proceed to his office at your convenience, to assist in his conversations with the other members of your party. Mam'selle!'

'Pray tell the Captain I shall join him in ten minutes,' Mary replied in a remarkably calm voice, considering that her mind and stomach were both churning with apprehension—perhaps even a touch of fear.

The Sergeant saluted himself out of the room, and Mr Brown rose, bade them all farewell as if he doubted if they would meet again in this world, and retired to his bed-chamber. Mary finished her coffee and then stood up.

Sir John, of course, also rose to his feet, and said anxiously, 'This is a great burden on you, m'dear, having to deal with this fellow. Wish I could relieve you of it—never had any facility with languages, though. Look here, you'll do your best to make what everyone says sound all right, from his point of view, won't you? The servants, I mean, for I suppose he means to question them, and you never know what silly things a servant might come out with when he's rattled! I'd lay odds that young Henry would swear he's longing to volunteer for the Navy if he's under any pressure!'

'Don't forget that the Captain understands English!' Mary replied. 'And I think it might be as well for us to take care what we say about him, for we can't be sure there isn't someone listening.'

'You think he'd set spies on us?' Sir John bridled at the idea.

'No, for I believe he's a gentleman, but this is an old building, and sometimes voices carry in such places. One of his men may overhear and report what we say to him—we don't know if he's the only one with a know-

ledge of English.' It sounded lame to Mary, who was
reluctant to admit that she had a very odd feeling that
Captain Dufour was as shadowy as he appeared when
she last saw him, and might well be present, unseen, in
almost any unlit corner or alcove, and there were plenty
of those in this old building, with its small windows and
myriad nooks and crannies. Less fancifully, she de-
plored the slighting manner in which Sir John referred to
the Captain—hardly tactful or sensible when they were
so completely at his mercy!

'See what you mean,' Sir John said thoughtfully, taking her point more sharply than she expected. 'You
understand, Sarah? No more referring to the fellow as a
fellow, or implying he ain't up to the mark in any way,
eh?'

'Very well, dear,' Lady Sarah replied equably, and
made a tiny grimace at Mary behind her husband's back.

Mary went up to her room, which was small and dark,
and carefully inspected herself as best she could in the
small mirror to see that her hair was tidy and her fresh
muslin gown uncrushed. She also collected a shawl, for,
in spite of the sunshine outside, it was distinctly cool in
the inn. Then she thought she had better delay no
longer, and set out to find the Captain.

She saw no-one on her way to his office. Even the door
of the room in which she had seen the soldiers last night
was closed, and the only sign of life was a distant voice
uplifted in unmelodious song, apparently across the yard
in the stables. She had no difficulty in finding her way,
but went straight to the correct door, tapped lightly, and
went in.

Captain Dufour was sitting at his desk, writing. He
glanced up as she entered, then put down his pen on the
inkstand, stood up and looked at her for a moment in
silence. One of the maids belonging to the inn was sitting
by the fireplace, sewing the long hem on a sheet, appar-

ently acting as a chaperone, but the Captain did not take the slightest notice of her, and she did not look up from her work.

'Good morning,' Mary said, as he did not speak.

'Good morning,' he replied. 'And pray allow me to congratulate you on your command of the French language.'

'Thank you.'

He continued to look at her for another moment, then appeared to recollect himself and invited her with a gesture to sit in the chair which she had occupied the previous evening. It had been moved a little to his left, so that he had to turn diagonally from his desk to face her as he resumed his seat. The bright morning light from the middle one of the three long windows fell on the left side of his face, unmercifully illuminating the ugly scars which disfigured it.

Mary tried not to look at them, but she was used to watching the eyes of the person to whom she was speaking, and it was difficult to focus entirely on his right eye. Her gaze kept straying to the black patch and the dull red scars which radiated from it, and each time she had to switch it back to the other eye, despite the uncertainty and confusion which its steady black regard aroused in her.

'If my disfigurement embarrasses you, pray feel free to turn away from me,' he said quietly, much as if he had suggested that the sun might be shining in her eyes.

As he was so direct and apparently unemotional about it, she replied honestly, 'It doesn't embarrass me, save that I naturally look at your face as we talk, and I don't wish to appear to be staring.'

'You need not concern yourself. One grows inured to being stared at, intentionally or accidentally.'

'I—I suppose a soldier must expect to be wounded, and so prepares himself for—for the eventuality . . .'

Mary stammered and tailed off, wishing she had not embarked on the sentence long before it was finished, for it sounded remarkably silly. How could any man prepare himself to expect disfigurement like that?

'A soldier expects it—a prisoner of war does not—at least, not among civilised peoples,' was the curt and bitter reply. Mary stared at him, puzzled, and actually opened her mouth to enquire what he meant, but he forestalled her by reverting to his usual dispassionate tones to say, 'I wish to hold a short conversation with each member of your party, and it would be helpful if you would assist me—to your advantage, also, as otherwise I should have to find an interpreter elsewhere, and that might take time.'

'I'm quite willing to help,' Mary replied quickly, thinking that another interpreter was unlikely to be English, and therefore might not translate correctly. It was quite another full second before it occurred to her that she might well make mistakes in her French which would change the meaning of what was said, and another second after that before she recalled that it was possible that he did not really need an interpreter at all, for he appeared to understand English perfectly well. Perhaps he used the device to set a barrier between himself and the person he was interrogating, or just to give himself more time to consider what they said.

'Shall we begin with you, then?' he asked, picking up his pen and laying aside the paper on which he had been writing. The desk apparently had drawers, for he reached down and produced another sheet of paper, on which he wrote Mary's name and the date. His handwriting was neat, and clear enough for her to be able to read it quite easily upside down, yet surprisingly quickly executed. She noticed that he spelled her Christian name in the English fashion, even if he did insist on pronouncing it in French.

He looked up, raised his eyebrows a fraction, and said, 'Talk to me about yourself, if you please.'

Mary began hesitantly to tell the story of her life, which took very little time as, apart from the death of her mother, her removal from London to Broadwood Magna while she was still in the nursery, and the death of her father, there was little to relate. Captain Dufour wrote notes, and, from time to time, she paused to let him catch up. During one of these pauses, she looked past his bent head and saw that the windows behind him looked out on a pretty garden, bounded by a high grey stone wall with a battlement walk-way. She realised with surprise that it must be the town wall, although she had gained the impression that the inn was in the middle of the town.

'Yes?' Captain Dufour prompted.

'Oh!' said Mary. 'I'm sorry—I was looking at the garden.'

The Captain twisted round in his chair and looked out of the window. 'One of the several charming idiosyncracies of Soleure. Many of the old houses have gardens hidden away behind them. Two of my men tend it—they were gardeners in civil life.'

Mary stood up and took a few steps towards the window to see better, and the Captain perforce rose as well.

'No doubt the original intention was to leave a clear space between the buildings and the wall, for military convenience,' he remarked, sounding a little more human than usual. Mary glanced up at him as she made some slight remark in reply, and saw his face in full light for the first time. He was younger than she had thought —certainly not more than thirty—and the lines on his face were those of pain, not age. His eye was not black at all, but a dark, velvety brown. Also, his expression was not so much sardonic as melancholy.

'Soleure seems to be a charming, quaint little town. It

must be a pleasant place to live, I should imagine?'

'I've known worse,' he replied, turning back to his desk. 'It's a busy place, with much coming and going, and consequently many passes to be issued and reports to write. Enough to provide occupation for an officer deemed unfit for active duty, even if the occupation is somewhat useless in itself.'

The bitter note was back in his voice, and Mary did not know how to answer him, so she went back to her seat and waited until he had resettled himself, thinking that he did not sound as if he enjoyed questioning people about their reasons for travelling, or interfering with their right to come and go as they pleased. However, he did not enlarge on the subject, but picked up his pen, inspected its point, and said in his usual cold manner, 'And how do you pass your time when you are at home?'

CHAPTER
THREE

MARY'S interview with Captain Dufour left her more than a little puzzled. For nearly an hour, he questioned her about her opinion on various matters, and he seemed particularly interested in the fact that she liked to read. He wanted to know what books she had read recently, and what she thought of them, and he appeared to have abandoned his note-taking by then, for he laid down his pen and sat back in his chair to listen. She had never, she thought, known anyone who could sit so still, for he hardly moved a muscle, even the eye fixed on her face rarely blinked, and his expression remained unchanged, set in a brooding, melancholy look.

Eventually, he thanked her with cold courtesy and enquired whether she would be willing to continue with another interview before lunch.

'As you please,' she replied.

'I've no wish to compel you, if you're fatigued.'

'I'm not at all fatigued, thank you,' she replied, trying to sound equally cold, and thinking that the sooner he had questioned everyone in the party, the sooner he would make his decision.

He picked up a little silver bell which stood by his inkstand, and shook it. The pretty tinkle it made had hardly died away when a soldier opened the door, and one of the inn-servants came in with a tray bearing a coffee-pot, three elegant cups and dishes, creamer and sugar basin. The pieces did not match, but the fact that they were porcelain marked the innkeeper's consciousness of the Captain's importance.

The servant poured coffee for Mary and handed her

the creamer, from which she took a spoonful, and the sugar, which she declined. The Captain took his coffee black and unsweetened, which Mary thought accorded well with his nature, although he thanked the servant, and sent him over to serve the silent chaperone with coffee before dismissing him. To the soldier, he simply said 'Fifteen minutes, Lebrun,' at which the man came to attention and withdrew after the servant, closing the door behind him.

There was silence for a few minutes, and Mary's eyes again strayed to the sunny garden outside the window.

'Are you thinking of marrying Mr Brown?' the Captain asked suddenly.

Mary started and almost dropped her cup. 'I . . .' she began. 'Really, I . . .' She made an effort to control the confusion into which the question had thrown her, and finally managed, 'The matter hasn't been mentioned.'

'You appear to lead a very dull life when you're at home, and offers of marriage don't come your way very frequently, one imagines? You must have thought about it.'

Mary felt her colour rising, and was tempted to try to snub him, but one look at that implacable face discouraged the idea completely, and she heard herself reply fairly calmly, '*If* he made me an offer, I would be foolish not to consider it.'

'You'd be foolish to accept!' he said briefly. 'May I offer you more coffee?'

'No, thank you.'

She put her cup and dish back on the tray, which had been left on his desk, and busied herself in untangling part of the fringe of her shawl. After a few more minutes of silence, a tap at the door heralded the reappearance of the soldier, Lebrun, with Mr Brown's valet, who was invited to sit by a gesture from the Captain. Lebrun took the tray out with him.

Captain Dufour questioned the valet for less than ten minutes. He was a plump, effeminate little man, obviously timid, for he jumped every time the Captain spoke, and twisted his hands together nervously as he listened to Mary's translation, then stammered when he answered. His eyes darted from the Captain to Mary and back again, giving him the look of a frightened rabbit, and Mary felt very sorry for him.

'You may go.' The Captain dismissed him abruptly when he had ascertained the man's age, how long he had been in Mr Brown's service, and what he thought about various political questions—to which the valet answered 'I d-don't know, really,' each time.

There was a pause when he had gone, and then Captain Dufour said in his usual dry fashion, 'I doubt if the Duke of York would find much use for him. Do you think he would faint if I showed him a musket?'

'You can't blame him for being afraid,' Mary said reprovingly. 'He only came abroad because his master wished to travel, and now he finds himself in danger of being locked up in prison for goodness knows how many years, depending on the whim of a man he doesn't know, and who frightens him.'

She then endured one of the Captain's silent stares, expecting some cutting whiplash of a riposte at the end of it, but he said quite mildly, 'Am I so intimidating? Do I frighten you?'

'Yes,' she admitted. 'Our fate hangs on you, yet to us you're an unknown quantity. We have good reason to fear you.'

'Yes,' was the only response. 'You need not translate the answers of my victims into French, only my questions,' and with that, he rang his bell again, and Lebrun brought in Sir John's valet, George.

Again, the interview was very brief. George was a quiet, thin little man, whose only interest, apart from his master's boots and clothes and his plan to marry Ellen one day, was the breeding of ferrets in partnership with Harry Cobb, the landlord of the Green Dragon in faraway Broadwood Magna. Mary had been unaware of this secret passion, which emerged only when the Captain asked him how he occupied his spare time, and was rewarded with a fanatical lecture on the *mustelidae*.

When he had withdrawn, the Captain enquired, 'Pray, what are ferrets?' and Mary was unable to answer briefly, as she did not know the French term. She tried to describe the animal, and the Captain listened soberly, but the muscle twitched by his mouth once or twice, and eventually he stood up and limped over to the bookshelves by the fireplace, which Mary had not noticed before. He was very lame, his right leg almost too weak to bear his weight, and his close-fitting trousers revealed, above the top of his half-boot, that his calf was badly mis-shapen.

'*Furet!*' he announced, shutting the book which he had been consulting and replacing it on the shelf. 'Does he perhaps train them to bite Frenchmen?'

He turned to look at Mary as he spoke, and, embarrassed at being caught staring at his leg, she replied at random that she believed the beasts needed no training to bite anyone, as they did it freely by the light of nature.

The Captain returned to his place and rang his bell again, and the interviews continued with the two coachmen, and then Ellen. Each was quite brief, and followed the same pattern as the questioning of the valets, except that he asked Ellen to describe her feelings about prisoners of war.

'I don't know what 'e means, Miss Mary!' the woman said in an agitated tone. ' 'Ow can I answer 'im if I don't know what 'e means?' Her usually quiet and refined speech had reverted to a shrill near-Cockney under stress.

'She's never come across a prisoner of war, and I don't expect she's ever thought about it,' Mary explained in French.

'Ask her, then, to think about it now, and tell me what she would feel if she did encounter such a person. Ask if she would still think of him as an enemy, even though he was a helpless prisoner.'

Puzzled, Mary relayed the question, and Ellen did her best to think about it, and then said 'Well, not if he was helpless. I'd show him Christian charity, I hope!'

Captain Dufour bent his head, and apparently inspected the back of his right hand, which was resting on the paper on which he was recording his notes. Mary saw that the hand was gripping his pen so tightly that the shaft of the quill had bent.

'Thank you. Tell her she may go,' he said abruptly, and Ellen left the room remarkably quickly for a middle-aged woman. He then spoke in German to the maid, who folded her sewing and left, still in silence, with a little bobbing curtsey.

Again, there was silence for a time as he read through what he had written, and then he sanded the sheet and added it to the small pile which had accumulated at his elbow. Turning to Mary, he said, 'Thank you for your assistance. I have other business to attend to this afternoon, but perhaps we might continue in the morning?'

'Yes, of course.'

'And perhaps you and your friends will dine with me this evening?'

Mary assumed that he intended some informal observation of them during the meal, so she thought it politic to accept, but she added, 'I doubt if Mr Brown will be available, however. He isn't at all well.'

'So I understand. No doubt I shall have the pleasure of his company when he is recovered.'

Mary hesitated for a moment, and then broke the

rather brooding silence which had again descended after
his last remark by saying, 'May I ask you something?'

'If you wish.'

She was tempted to ask him why he was so concerned
—almost obsessional, she felt—about prisoners of war,
but thought fleetingly that it might be unwise. After all,
he had only mentioned the subject twice, in fact, so
perhaps she was mistaken in thinking it had some significance, and if it had, she might antagonise him by asking
about it. Rather than make herself look foolish by deciding not to ask anything after all, she switched to something else which had caught her attention. 'Last night,
when I mentioned the First Consul—when I said that we
were acquainted with him—you offered your commiserations. What did you mean?'

'Do you know him well?' he countered.

'No,' she admitted. 'We were presented to him at a
ball in Paris. He hardly spoke.'

The Captain considered his answer, leaning back in
his chair and staring straight in front of him. 'One cannot
admire a General who abandons his army when it's
plague-stricken and demoralised, to pursue his own political ambitions. One may, perhaps, accept that the need
of France was greater at the time, but one would expect
that he might at least make some provision for them, or
even enquire after their welfare from time to time. That,
of course, is a treasonable statement, so it will do no
more harm if I add that, in my opinion, General Bonaparte is an ill-mannered, self-opinionated little Corsican
upstart, who unfortunately also happens to be a genius.
As one of your American cousins once remarked, "if
that be treason, make the most of it"! I should deny
having said it if you tried, of course!'

'Naturally,' Mary replied, determined not show surprise in face of his unruffled calm. 'I look forward to
seeing you at dinner, then,' and with that blatant un-

truth, she rose to her feet and made her exit. A clatter from the desk indicated that he had knocked over his stick as he stood up, but she refrained from glancing back.

She found Lady Sarah and Sir John in the parlour, in immediate expectation of lunch. They greeted her as if she had made an unexpected escape from the Castle of Giant Despair, and she was amused to find herself actually defending Captain Dufour from their criticisms, assuring them that he had been perfectly civil and not at all threatening in his manner. They were dubious about the invitation to dine, but saw the sense of Mary's argument that it would be wise to fall in with the Captain's wishes, as so much depended on his opinion.

'It's quite iniquitous that such should be the case!' grumbled Lady Sarah.

'Indeed, but at least he seems to be trying to form a fair judgment,' Mary pointed out. 'After all, he could simply take the line that all English travellers are to be interned, and I don't suppose his superiors would find fault with such an attitude. As it is, he seems to take each case on its merits, and I suppose he will then have to justify his decision to Paris.'

'Yes, I suppose you're right,' Sir John admitted grudgingly. 'I gather from Johann that this fell—man's predecessor was a very different sort—made unnecessary difficulties for everyone, and was thoroughly disliked for it. Ah, well—we'd best dine with him and maintain the civilities!'

'Is there any news of poor Mr Brown?' Mary enquired over lunch.

'A doctor came to see him, and assured him that he has only a heavy head-cold,' Lady Sarah replied. 'He sent round a draught to help soothe his throat, and advised him to spend a day or two in his room. I do hope we may not all have taken the infection from him!'

After coffee, Mary fetched her embroidery from her room and sat stitching it at the table with Lady Sarah. Sir John read a book, in the intervals of fidgetting about, and presently found better entertainment, for a trickle of people began to arrive at the inn, apparently seeking permits to travel, and the parlour window provided an excellent view of them. Sir John kept up a running commentary for the benefit of the ladies, making up a variety of unlikely tales to fit the appearance of the individuals, endowing one with a sick relative with a fortune to bestow, another with a wedding to attend, a third with a bankruptcy to avert, and any number of other reasons for leaving the town.

Sergeant Girard made an appearance during the afternoon to enquire if they had any pressing needs, and Mary took the opportunity to ask him about the people.

'I suppose they are seeking passes to leave the town?' she said.

'Yes, mam'selle. It being a garrison town, anyone wishing to enter or leave needs a small pass. Anyone wanting to cross the frontier into France or Vaud or Austria, or the Italian Republic, needs a bigger pass.'

'And Baden?' Mary enquired, not with any particular purpose, but because he had omitted that country.

'Not Baden. The Germans don't seem to mind who crosses their frontier, mam'selle, so long as they've a passport. Bâle is a very open city, you see, and you can't really tell which country you're in as you go about the streets.'

After he had gone, Sir John lost interest in the passing show and returned to his book. Mary wasted a little time in fruitless regrets that they had ever entered Soleure, for it seemed that the Bavarians had been right, and if they had crossed the Aare somewhere else, they might have slipped through Bâle and could now have been travelling freely across the German states. To divert

herself from the squirrel-in-a-cage frame of mind induced by such thoughts, she drifted into one of her
daydreams, or, rather, a series of them.

First, she imagined herself soothing the fevered brow
of a much more sick Mr Brown, and earning his fervent
admiration for her devoted nursing, but this picture was
not particularly pleasing, as she knew very well that he
had only a cold, and she had really become a little weary
of his sheep's eyes and indifferent poetry.

Her thoughts drifted to Captain Dufour, and she wondered how he had come by his injuries. Putting together
his comment on them, and his questions to Ellen, she
concluded that either his face or his leg had been
wounded while he was a prisoner, which seemed an
extraordinary and disturbing thought. Half-unconsciously, she imagined herself nursing the Captain, and
reached a point where he was smiling at her and thanking her for saving his life with a fervency so unlike his
actual reserved and unemotional manner that she was
jerked back to reality by the sheer incongruity of it. She
was surprised, on reflection, to find that this picture had
been far more satisfactory than the previous one, but she
dismissed that with the acknowledgement that she had
always cherished a preference for tall, dark men, and the
Captain had probably been handsome before . . . Poor
man!

'Who is, dear?' enquired Lady Sarah. 'You said "Poor
man!" ' as Mary looked startled. 'If it's Mr Brown, I
don't think you need worry—he takes very good care of
himself!'

'Yes, I . . .' Mary hesitated, and then went on, 'I was
thinking of Captain Dufour, in fact.'

'Oh,' Lady Sarah was disconcerted, but she soon rallied, and commented, 'Yes, I suppose he must have
suffered a great deal—any injury to the eye is so painful,
and he appears to be rather lame, as well.'

After a little more desultory conversation, Lady Sarah
fell into a light doze, whence her husband had preceded
her, and Mary, not wishing to dwell any longer on the
dark and enigmatic figure of Captain Dufour, began to
think back over her experiences of the past year. Broadwood now seemed very remote, and she recognised that
she herself had changed in many ways, but at the moment, she very much wished herself back in that quiet
haven, so far away in distance and time, although life
there would seem so very dull after travelling and meeting people. Once back at the Brick House at Broadwood
Magna, she would have no escape from monotony but
her daydreams, and it was only now that she realised
how little she had resorted to them in the past twelve-
month. Where they had formerly been a major occupation, they had now become only a pleasant means of
passing an idle hour, and even there, could easily be
replaced by reliving the scenes and conversations of her
travels.

She recalled the pleasant strolls along the sands at
Cannes, the mingled scents of lavender, fish, seaweed,
and pinetrees, the tortuous shapes of the olive trees, the
warm sea-breeze, the brilliant blue of sea and sky. It was
easy to recapture the view from the harbour, which she
had sketched a dozen times, looking towards the Îles des
Lérins, where, local legend claimed, a mysterious prisoner had once been kept, with a mask of iron over his
face, either as a punishment, or to hide his identity from
his gaolers.

Captain Dufour was like that, she mused. He wore the
mask of his own face, hiding his thoughts and emotions,
so that no-one could know his character, and that was
why he was such a frightening person. No, not frightening—more disturbing, intriguing, for one could not help
wondering what he was thinking and feeling, whether he
was really as cold and unemotional as he appeared.

'Really!' she thought. 'Everything seems to bring me back to that man! I'm becoming obsessional about him! It's the uncertainty, of course, not knowing what will become of us, and everything resting on his decision. Perhaps he'll say something about it at dinner.'

However, the Captain said very little about anything at dinner. The meal was served in the room next door to his office, with a similar scrubbed plank floor, a fireplace which obviously shared the same chimney, and similar long dark velvet curtains. It was a narrower room, furnished with a square oak table and heavy, old-fashioned chairs with surprisingly comfortable saddle-seats, and a court-cupboard decorated with maiolica plates and dishes from the same set as those in his office. Mr Brown still being indisposed, they sat one on each side of the table, with the only light provided by a four-branched candelabrum, which stood off-centre on the table, nearer to Sir John than to the Captain, who sat opposite him, so that the latter was outside the circle of light which it cast, and seemed half-withdrawn into the shadows. He followed the conversation, which was in English, but his few remarks were in French, and perforce directed to Mary, who was seated on his left, each time with a polite request that she translate what he said to the appropriate person. It did not make for sparkling conversation.

Long before the main course was finished, Mary had an uneasy feeling, reminiscent, she thought, of Macbeth at the banquet, that the Captain was possibly not there in the flesh at all, for he seemed no more than a shadowy figure, a presence observing them from another dimension. This was partly due to the fact that his dark uniform was almost invisible in the dim light, and the side of his face nearest to her partially obscured by his eyepatch, but also to the difficulty Sir John and Lady Sarah found in including him in the conversation. They tried at first,

as good manners demanded, addressing him in a normal
manner, but the awkwardness of receiving his replies
indirectly, through Mary, and the possible inconveni-
ence to her of having to perform this service, obviously
made it a burdensome business, and gradually they said
less and less to him, until eventually they were only
keeping up a gentle flow of small-talk around three sides
of the table, with the fourth person silent, listening, and,
like Banquo's ghost, causing a feeling of unease in at
least one of those present.

All in all, Mary could not feel that the dinner-party
was a success, although the food was very good and
nothing untoward occurred. When at last it was over, the
Captain bade them 'Goodnight' in pleasant tones, and
Sir John commented on the way upstairs that he was a
gentlemanly fellow, and surely not likely to take an
uncivilised attitude about the internment business.

Mary felt unable to share this optimism. In her own
room, she sat on the edge of her bed and tried to imagine
herself into the Captain's side of the question, attempt-
ing to see the morning's conversations with the servants
and herself from his point of view, but soon found that
she could not even imagine the point of view of a man
who revealed so little of himself, and, instead, lapsed
into idle fancies of herself making some brilliant observation which would prove irrefutably to the Captain that
he should allow them to go on their way, or, alterna-
tively, of rescuing her companions from their predicament by some noble act of self-sacrifice. Nothing
practical suggested itself, apart from prayer, so eventually she composed herself to try to sleep, with the not
very comforting thought that the morning might bring
the answer.

It did not. To begin with, Mr Brown's valet reported
that his master, although a little better, did not feel
sufficiently up to the mark to leave his room, and then

Lady Sarah declared in tones of gentle resignation that her throat felt uncomfortably sore, and perhaps Mary would be so kind as to request Sergeant Girard to send to the doctor for a soothing draught.

The Sergeant appeared while they were still at breakfast, and having made his formal greeting and request for orders, stood himself at ease and relaxed into a sympathetic attitude and undertook to despatch an orderly forthwith, recommending, meanwhile, a concoction of honey, thyme and hyssop which his old granny had sworn by, and which Johann could mix in next to no time at all. He then reverted to his more military manner, and presented to Mary the Captain's apologies and regrets that he had been called away on business, and was not sure at what hour he would return, and begged her indulgence to continue his interviews the following day.

Mary naturally made the responses required by courtesy, but she regretted the postponement, partly because it meant further delay and continued uncertainty, but also because the prospect of a long, dull day now stretched before her, and she was tired of sitting at her embroidery. If only she could go out for a walk!

The morning passed very slowly, and was not helped by the unpleasant thought that, if she were to be interned, presumably there would be years to endure of long, long days with nothing to do, cooped up indoors, unable to feel the wind and rain on her face . . . surely she would go mad!

After lunch, Lady Sarah decided that the Sergeant's concoction had helped her throat to some extent, and that she might now be able to make good some of the sleep it had caused her to lose during the night, so she retired upstairs. Sir John wandered off to the stables to see the horses and talk to William and Henry, no doubt feeling a need for masculine company after a day and a half of almost exclusively female society, so Mary was left alone in the parlour, yawning, sewing, fidgetting, feeling the room become steadily more and more stuffy.

There were not even any applicants for passes to watch, as they were being stopped at the outer gate, apparently leaving their names with the soldier on guard. A little sunlight fell into the courtyard, but it only served to make the room seem more chill and gloomy, and eventually, Mary became too restless to sit still any longer.

'If I can't go out, I'll take a walk indoors!' she thought, and went out into the hall.

There was no-one about, no sound of life from inside the building, so she walked across to the passage which led towards the Captain's office, moving silently in her soft slippers. The door of the room where the soldiers sat—the guard-room, she supposed—was closed, so she crept past it, and reached the turn of the passage in a rush, then paused to listen. Not a sound.

Somewhere along here must be a door to the garden. If she could find it, she could at least look out and see the sky and a little greenery, and get a breath of air. She moved along slowly, peering cautiously out of each of the windows to the courtyard before darting past it. There was only the guard at the gate in sight, and he was standing on the street side of the arch, with his back towards her.

She passed the Captain's office, the dining-room, then another door, and found herself approaching the foot of a staircase to the upper floor. Just before it came an opening, and she crept up to the corner, listening and watching for any sign of life from the stairs, or the passage which continued beyond it. Still there was no sound. She peered round the corner into the opening. It was a mere five or six yards long, and led to the garden door.

It was bolted, but not locked, and the bolts moved freely and silently, so in a moment she had the door open. Its hinges squealed a little, and she held her breath and froze, waiting for someone to come to investigate the noise. Nothing. She stepped forward into the recess —too slight to be called a porch—and looked out at the garden, which was quite small, little more than a hundred paces across and as much again in width, bounded on the left by a low wall, and on the right by the back of a long, low building.

The arrangement was quite formal, with a path running all round the edge, and two more crossing at right angles in the middle, and a fountain at the intersection. Between the paths were rectangles of grass and formal beds planted with small shrubs and edged with pansies and forgetmenots. Some of the shrubs were roses, just coming into flower.

Mary looked carefully about her, but there was no sign of anyone. This side of the garden was in the shadow of the inn, for it lay to the east of the building, but the afternoon sun fell diagonally across the far side, bathing the high grey town wall in golden light. She looked at it longingly for a moment, then walked resolutely as far as the fountain.

It was not playing, but the basin was full of water on which floated a few lily-pads, and the reddish-gold shapes of fish could be seen in the green depths. She dabbled her fingers in the water and admired the greeny-bronze figure in the middle. It was a boy riding on a dolphin, and was designed to spout water from the mouth of the curving creature and from the shell which the boy held poised above his head.

Beyond the fountain, the path led to a flight of steps, cut into the face of the town wall and giving access to the battlement walk. Mary glanced back at the building behind her. The windows were blind, half of them shuttered. Nothing moved. Quickly, she skirted the fountain and ran to the steps, which were steep and a trifle slippery, but she climbed them safely, steadying herself with a hand on the wall, and stood at the top, looking about her.

Level with the boundaries of the garden, the walk was closed off by iron grills, padlocked to staples set in the wall. Looking down on the garden, she saw that beyond the low wall was a yard stacked with boxes and barrels in various sizes, all very new-looking, and the building which formed the other boundary was a stable or outhouse in the yard of the narrow house next door. Beyond the steep roofs, as she looked a little to her right, she could see the Baroque curves and domes of a great church, which she assumed must be the Cathedral.

She turned and craned to see over the wall. By standing on tiptoe, she could just manage it, and found a fine view spread before her. She could not see what lay directly below where she stood, of course, so she could not ascertain if there were any buildings there, but it seemed that there were few houses outside the wall on this side of the town. To her right, the river flowed out of the town and receded into the far distance, meandering gently down a wide valley until it disappeared into the haze, from which rose a distant range of mountains. There were more mountains to the left, not high enough to be snow-capped. Their green slopes were dotted with herds of cattle, little farm-houses, clumps of dark trees. Mary realised that they must be the Jura.

Across the river, the ground rose in range upon range of rolling hills, until, on the far horizon, she could see the bright gleam of snow caps. On the nearer hills, too, were grazing cattle, farms, trees, little villages.

Some way along the wall to her left, there appeared to be one or two towers, close together and projecting outward from the town, and she could see that this must be a gateway, for a road ran out from that point, as far as she could ascertain by jumping up and scrabbling her toes against the wall. She could trace the line of the road quite clearly. It swung away from the river almost as it left the town, and followed the edge of the Jura as far as she could follow it, until it went out of sight behind a projecting hill, its course marked by a line of trees. She wondered where it went, and after a little thought, decided that it was probably the road to Bâle—the road which she and her friends soon hoped to take away from this place.

It was very pleasant up here on the wall, with the sun warming her back and illuminating the fine scene before her, although she could wish the wall were three inches lower, or herself three inches taller, so that she did not have to stretch so much to see over it. Presumably it was the right height above the walkway to protect a defender, whilst still allowing him to see over, provided that he was as tall as Sir John or Captain Dufour—Mr Brown would be little better off than herself in that respect.

A barge swam into sight on the river, gliding smoothly, with a fan of ripples spreading behind it. A big white horse was plodding along the bank, towing it on a line without any sign of effort, presumably going downstream, and the whole thing seemed to be managed by two boys, one riding the horse and the other sitting on the stern of the barge with one foot on the tiller. She wondered where they were going, and what cargo the barge carried under its canvas cover.

How very pleasant it was to stand here, leaning against the cool grey stone, with a slight breeze stirring her hair! Much better than that stuffy, dull little parlour! At least here she could breathe the fresh, clean air and watch whatever was passing on the road or river, and admire the fine view. It was quiet, too. Some birds were

singing in the trees down there, outside the wall, and
a blackbird was trilling in the garden behind her. The
breeze carried the scent of warm grass and flowers, and
the distant sound of voices and rumbling wheels from the
cobbled streets of the town behind her.

Suddenly, there was something else—a nearer sound
—a squeal, like door-hinges in need of oil—familiar . . .

She turned and looked down into the garden. At first,
she saw no-one, and thought that she was mistaken, and
then a slight movement caught her eye, and she realised
that Captain Dufour was standing in the dark oblong of
the open doorway, looking up at her. She could almost
feel his eye upon her, and she shivered and pressed
herself back against the wall, stretching out her hands on
either side to steady herself.

For a few seconds, nothing moved. The blackbird had
stopped singing and was perched on the edge of the basin
of the fountain. Suddenly, he dipped his head and threw
sparkling drops of water over his back, fluttering his
wings. The Captain stepped out into the garden and
began to make his halting way towards Mary. The bird
flew away at his approach.

CHAPTER
FOUR

MARY watched the Captain like a mesmerised rabbit as he slowly crossed the garden, one part of her mind feeling sorry for his lameness, but most of her thoughts running around the fear that he would be angry, that by her selfish desire to come out of the inn, she might have condemned them all to internment. Would he punish her? She felt quite sick with apprehension as he drew nearer.

He walked with his head slightly bent, keeping his gaze on the path, until he reached the foot of the steps, and then he paused for a moment and looked up. Mary shivered again and tried to swallow the lump which had risen in her throat. She was unconsciously pressing herself harder against the stone at her back, as if her body wished to vanish into the wall. His face was as inscrutable as ever.

As he started to mount the steps, she managed to turn her head a little to one side, to avoid watching him, for he clearly found the climb difficult and taxing. His right leg had to be braced by his stick, and his shoulder against the wall, and he took each step, one at a time, leading with his left foot, and she felt that he might resent her appearing to watch his painful progress. She could hear him catching his breath at each effort as she kept her eyes on the pavé at her feet, and then a black shadow fell across the stones, and a cautious, sidelong glance showed her that he was standing beside her.

'I wasn't trying to find a means of escape,' she said unsteadily, sounding frightened and defensive.

'You would need one of M. Garnerin's balloons for

that,' he replied quietly. 'Unless you managed to scramble over the garden wall into the yard next door, which belongs to a cooper and boxmaker. You could then hide in one of his barrels, I suppose, until I sent my trained wolves to sniff you out.'

'Wolves!' exclaimed Mary in alarm.

'Naturally. A practical method of dealing with escaping internees. The wolves find the escaper and eat him— or her—and that saves the expense both of feeding the wolves and of lodging and feeding the captured escaper. The English are not the only ingenious people in Europe, you know—the French have a few clever ideas as well!'

Mary regarded him obliquely for a few moments. He was using the advantage of his height to look out over the wall with apparent interest, and she thought that he was probably joking, in his sardonic fashion.

'I—I shouldn't care to be eaten by wolves!' she ventured.

'They would do it quite efficiently—no mess to clear up afterwards, apart from a little blood. They find a young and tender female much to their taste, I believe.'

Mary managed an unconvincing laugh, and then said soberly, 'I expect you are angry with me for coming into your garden, but it was so dull and stuffy in the parlour. I'm not accustomed to remaining indoors all day.'

'You may have to become accustomed to it,' was the cold reply.

'None of the others knows that I'm here—please don't blame them for my misdemeanour!'

'You don't wish your friends to be eaten?' He glanced at her as he spoke, and then looked at the view again.

'I meant, please don't let my thoughtless behaviour affect your decision about—about their fate!'

He sighed faintly, and then said thoughtfully, 'The matter presents a personal problem. I have a consider-

able score to settle with the English, and it's tempting—
very tempting—when I find myself with a chance to pay
it off! If it were otherwise, it would be easy to give you
all passes and let you go, or send you all to internment,
but whichever I do, I shall always wonder if I freed you
in reaction against my desire for vengeance, or imprisoned you in order to satisfy it.'

'Surely you wouldn't take vengeance on helpless
women?' Mary ventured, and immediately regretted it,
for he rounded on her with a sudden blaze of fury.

'Helpless?' he snarled. 'My God! You don't know
what you say! It was a helpless woman and helpless
children who destroyed my eye!'

Mary shrank back, frightened, and whispered 'I—I'm
sorry . . .'

'You have good reason to be!' he said more calmly,
looking at her white face and puzzled eyes. 'Perhaps I
should explain, as you are somewhat concerned in the
matter. No doubt you recall the English and Russian
invasion of the Batavian Republic in '99?'

'The Helder Expedition. Yes.'

'I was taken prisoner in the course of it, and sent
across to England. It happened that I was the only officer
in that particular shipload of prisoners, so at Harwich, I
was separated from the others, put in a closed carriage,
and sent with an escort of four soldiers to the camp at
Norman Cross. We went by quiet roads, for two days
and nights, sleeping in the coach for a few hours at night
and stopping at village inns for food, which the guards
made me eat in the coach, without untying my hands,
although I'd given my parole—apparently they didn't
consider an officer of the Revolutionary Army to be a
gentleman.

'By the second morning, I was very weary of the
stuffy, smelly coach, and begged them to let me out, so
when we stopped for a meal, they kindly relented and

fastened me between two convenient staples in the outer wall of the building, so . . .' He stretched out his arms to their full extent on either side.

'You can see that a man tied by the wrists in that manner can't defend himself. They went inside, and, a few minutes later, the village children found me. Helpless, innocent little English children! They jeered, and then began to pelt me with whatever came to hand—mud, filth, stones—and I could do nothing! Then a woman came along, a young woman, pretty, neatly dressed—much like you in appearance, though not of your class. I called to her, thinking that she would help me, but she only laughed, and then egged on the children to throw more, while she mocked at me.' His voice sounded oddly impersonal, both now and later, as if he were only reporting something which had happened to someone else, and meant nothing much to him, except for a certain dry, restrained bitterness.

'Then one of the boys found a bottle. He stood with it in his hands, half wanting to throw it, half afraid of the consequences, and the woman screamed at him, but not to stop him! No, she wanted him to throw it, so he did, but it just missed my head and smashed against the wall. Then the children scattered and ran, but the woman seized the broken-off neck, and slashed the jagged edge hard across my face, twice.'

He pulled off his eye-patch, and Mary saw with sick horror that there were two vicious scars criss-crossing the empty eye-socket, and it was quite clear how the jagged glass had torn across his face.

'I suppose I screamed,' he went on calmly, only the slightest unsteadiness in his voice, and even that was soon brought under control. 'The guards came running out, but the woman had run out of sight. They were kind to me, in their rough way. They took me inside the inn and gave me brandy, and a pad of clean linen to put over the injury, and I think they debated whether they should try to find a doctor—I knew very little English then, and I was in no state to take in much of what they were saying—but, in the event, we went on to Norman Cross, where one of my compatriots who had some medical training removed what was left of my eye, and stitched the wounds. Don't speak to me of helpless English-women!'

Mary was silent, and felt her eyes fill with tears at the shock and horror of his story. She had heard a few tales of cruelty by women, but never concerning an ordinary English woman in an ordinary village at home, nor first hand from the victim.

'After a year in the camp, I grew tired of being caged,' he went on in a reflective tone. 'You can, perhaps, understand that, after a day in a stuffy room, with no-thing very much to do.' Mary felt quite as ashamed as he probably intended. 'It was foolish and hopeless, of course, to try to escape from an island in the sea, in a shabby, but unmistakably French uniform, and although I had learned to speak English, my accent was not typical of a native! I suppose I was a little mad by then—I suspect that I still am, in some respects—and it seemed better to try . . . It wasn't difficult to get away from the camp, but after three days of running and hiding, I was wet, cold, hungry, and so tired that I fell asleep in a straw-stack, and when I woke, two of your militia-man were standing over me. Like a fool, I tried to run, and one of them shot me in the leg to discourage me, and broke both bones in my calf. Then they dragged me to a magistrate—just such a man as your friend, Sir John—and he locked me in his cellar while he sent to Norman Cross for guards to take me back. He gave me food and water, but no light or air, and nothing to dress my wound. I had to tear up my shirt and bandage my leg as best I could, in the darkness, and to get my food and water, I had to find the cellar steps and crawl up them to seek for it, unable to see my hand before my face.'

'With a broken leg?' Mary exclaimed in horror.

'Perhaps you can understand why the bones didn't knit very well. I believe I was three days in that cellar. I was ill with fever for some weeks after that, and then I behaved myself in a proper manner until Peace was signed, and I came home, unfit for active duty.'

Mary was silent for a time, and then said tremulously, 'I can see why you hate the English so much.'

'They say that the French are a vindictive people, very prone to take vengeance,' was the cold, impersonal reply. Mary took a blurred look at him, blinked to clear her sight, and saw that he was contemplating the view again with as much emotion visible on his face as if he had been discussing the weather, or the price of hay. As if he could feel her eyes on him, he gave her one brief glance, and then replaced his eye-patch and resumed his contemplation of the view.

'I . . . I don't know what to say . . .' she stammered timidly. 'I'm ashamed, and sorry . . .'

He turned to look at her again, no more than a movement of the head, and he might as well have been glancing at a specimen in a museum, without feeling or interest, and then said abruptly, 'You may come into the garden when you please, and up here as well, but pray do not bring Sir John or Mr Brown with you. The door is locked at sunset, and Sergeant Girard keeps the key.'

'Thank you!' she croaked, so surprised that she seemed to have lost her voice, but found herself addressing his back, for he had turned and was about to descend the steps. Each stumbling, difficult step seemed to jar through her own body as she reflected on the suffering which lay behind his unemotional account. She longed to go after him, to call to him, to say something, but what? Any expression of pity or regret would only sound as if she were trying to ingratiate herself, to affect his decision regarding her future.

Nevertheless, as he reached the bottom of the steps, she said, 'Captain Dufour!' He stopped and turned to look up at her. For a second, at least, they stared at each other in silence, then he said prosaically, 'I regret that I had to abandon you this morning. Perhaps we may continue the interviews in the morning, if Lady Sarah and Mr Brown are well enough.'

Her eyes filled again, and as he finished speaking, two large tears welled over and ran down her cheeks. He seemed almost to wince, and then he made her a slight bow, as if to acknowledge what she had been unable to say, and turned to go back across the garden. He paused for a moment by the fountain, and stood looking down into the water, then limped on to the door and disappeared into the inn.

Mary watched until he had gone, then turned towards the wall and let the tears flow unchecked, not at all sure why she was crying—was it for him, for his bitterness, for his suffering—or was it for fear of what they might do to her own life and the lives of her friends? She thought she could at least imagine something of how he must feel towards English people, and how could she blame him for hating a nation which had treated him so? She leaned her head against the cold stone and sobbed until the storm of misery passed, and left her feeling drained and wretched.

When she raised her head and sought in her reticule for a handkerchief to dry her cheeks, it seemed odd that nothing beyond the wall had changed. The valley still lay sparkling and bright, like a fresh oil-painting, in the sunshine and clear air. A cart was just setting out along the road behind a pair of strong bay horses, driven by a man in a broad-brimmed straw hat. Another barge was gliding along the river, towards the town this time, its

towing horse leaning hard into his collar against the drag
of the current. Behind her in the garden, the blackbird
was trilling again. For all that the rest of the world cared,
she and Captain Dufour might have been a couple of
ants which happened to have met on the wall, and nothing of what had happened to him, or might happen to
her, meant any more to the carter or the bargemen than
if those ants had been brushed aside into oblivion. If she
were sent into internment tomorrow, the river would
still flow, and the scene before her would still slumber
peacefully in the sun.

Did the woman who had half-blinded him ever think
of what she had done, and perhaps feel some remorse?
Presumably she had some reason for doing it—perhaps
her husband had been killed in the war . . . It was
frightening to see how one action could set off a whole
train of circumstances which would eventually involve so
many other people . . .

She stayed on the wall, thinking and praying, until the
sun dropped behind the roof of the inn, and the shadow
of the building fell across her, making her shiver at the
sudden chill. As she turned to go down the steps, a clock
began to chime, probably from the Cathedral, and another joined in at a greater distance. She counted the
strokes, and was surprised to hear five—she must have
been here in the garden for more than two hours.

As she walked along the passage past Captain
Dufour's office, Sergeant Girard came out of it. She
bade him 'Good afternoon,' and added a trifle defensively, 'Your Captain said I might go into the garden.'

'Indeed, mam'selle,' he agreed politely. 'It's very
pleasant out there. Quite a little haven.'

She smiled, and he gave her a friendly, benevolent
look, and fell into step beside her as she continued on
her way round the corner.

'I suppose you must find it rather dull here, for a

soldier,' she ventured. 'Just dealing with people wanting to travel, I mean.'

'Not dull, mam'selle. This is a pleasant little town, like my own home, and the folk are friendly. They don't mind us, because they're used to Frenchmen being about. Our Ambassador to the cantons had his residence here for a couple of hundred years, you know. The folk who come for passes are interesting too, though they sometimes get a bit disagreeable if they have to wait about. The Captain tries to be fair, and he doesn't often have to refuse them. Mind you, the officer who was here before him wasn't very popular, Very set against the Swiss, he was, and made enemies. Captain Dufour gets on well with the townsfolk, and that makes things better for us. It's not as exciting as campaigning, but I've had near thirty years of that, man and boy, and don't pine to go back to it!'

Mary was a little surprised by his easy manner, particularly the way he spoke about his officer, and really might be said to have criticised the Captain's predecessor, but she supposed that a Revolutionary Army would differ considerably from the British variety in such matters. 'Thirty years!' she exclaimed. 'You must have started very young!'

'Sixteen, I was. There were twelve of us children at home, you see, mam'selle, and never enough to eat, nor decent clothes. In the army, you get food and good boots and a uniform, most of the time, at least, and you see a bit of the world.'

'Yes. I suppose you must have travelled a great deal.'

'I've been in America, and the Low Countries, and Italy, and Germany, and Egypt,' he said proudly. 'I got plague in Syria, and lucky to be alive after it, but one of the doctors felt sorry for the men in my tent—he thought we were all sure to die, so he gave us enough laudanum to put us out of our misery, and instead of that, most of us got better! It left us a lot weaker though, so that's why I'm here now—not considered strong enough for active duty. Still, it could be a lot worse!'

They had reached the door of what Mary thought of as the Soldiers' Room, and he had stopped there, pausing to finish what he was saying, before giving her a smart salute and a polite, 'I've enjoyed talking to you, mam'selle,' and going inside.

Mary continued to the parlour, where she found Sir John, changed for dinner, reading his book by the window.

'Ah, there you are!' he exclaimed as he got up. 'Couldn't think where you'd got to. Sarah's coming down in a minute—says she feels better now, thanks to that stuff the Sergeant got mixed up for her.'

'Oh, I'm so glad!' replied Mary. 'I'll go up and change.'

She washed her face and put on a blue silk dress, as the evenings were a little chilly here for muslin, then brushed her hair and pinned it up again, surveying herself in the small mirror to see how she looked. Even her own modest assessment admitted that she was not unattractive, and she thought to herself that it would be very pleasant to move in a more lively society than she would ever find in Broadwood Magna, and perhaps find a man who would appreciate her looks and modest fortune enough to marry her. She would very much like to have a husband and children, and a pretty house, perhaps in a town, where she might entertain friends to tea and give small dinner-parties, and go out in turn to other houses, and perhaps even to concerts and assemblies. How pleasant it would be to have a family to occupy her time, and interesting people to talk to, so that she would not be obliged to invent things to do to pass the days, or fritter them away in idle daydreaming—as she was doing now, she realised, with a guilty little grimace at her reflection.

Lady Sarah was already down when she returned to the parlour, and so, to everyone's surprise, was Mr Brown. He replied to Mary's polite enquiry with a somewhat lengthy account of his sufferings, which, in Mary's ears, formed a painful contrast to Captain Dufour's quiet account of his dreadful experiences. She was consequently not as generous with expressions of concern as Lady Sarah, who naturally felt obliged to give a parallel account of her own disagreeable hours with her sore throat. Between them, they took up most of the conversation while dinner was served and eaten, and, when the table had been cleared, Sir John produced a pack of cards, and hopefully suggested a few hands of loo, which passed the evening until bedtime.

In the morning, Sergeant Girard appeared after breakfast with his usual enquiry after their needs, and then conveyed an invitation from the Captain to Mary and Lady Sarah to go to his office, at their convenience. Lady Sarah was a trifle nervous of the idea, and insisted on returning to her room first, to tidy herself. She reappeared a good half-hour later in a different dress and clutching a vinaigrette, to which she had frequent recourse as she walked with Mary along the passage to the office.

The Captain was standing by the window as they entered, a dark, still figure against the morning sunlight, which fell diagonally across his desk, yet seemed not to illuminate him at all. The maid with her sewing was sitting by the fireplace again, head bent and absorbed in her work, and a sheet of paper lay ready on the desk, with the dictionary which the Captain had used to translate 'ferret' beside it. He greeted them in his usual coldly courteous fashion, and invited them to be seated.

Lady Sarah dropped her reticule, bent to retrieve it,

and dropped her vinaigrette, which somehow slid away across the floor. The Captain naturally went to retrieve it, and, although he usually seemed able to manage such a short distance without his stick, this time he appeared to stumble slightly as he held out the little silver box to Lady Sarah, his leg gave way, and he had to catch at the desk to save himself. Mary started up in an instinctive move to help him, then subsided again as she saw it was not necessary, and there was a sudden feeling of embarrassed constraint for a moment, which Lady Sarah broke by making a fluttering little speech of thanks for his attention.

'If we may begin,' he said when she had finished, and sat down in his place.

Lady Sarah's examination was quite brief. He asked her why she had decided to spend so long in France, to which she replied that the English winter was so harsh that her physician had always advised her to avoid it if she could, and that she had always wintered abroad in former days, and had longed for many years to see all her favourite places again.

He then asked her if she had found France much changed, and seemed interested in her comments, which were sensible and tactful, for she made no mention of bad roads, surly innkeepers and dirty inns, neglected, ruined churches and mansions, upstart officials, or the many missing faces from her former circle of acquaintance in Paris, dwelling only on the improvements she had noticed, and tailing off with a vague, 'and, oh, so many things are different, it is impossible to give account of all of them!' when her list proved woefully short. She even managed to recall a little of her almost forgotten French, which she must once have spoken quite well.

He next enquired how she spent her time at home in England, and received a catalogue of trivial occupations which she finished with an apologetic, 'My health is so uncertain, you see, that I dare not exert myself too much, so I live very quietly.'

'Indeed,' he replied non-committally, then thanked her courteously and rang his little bell for the waiting orderly. It was not Lebrun, but an older man called Martin, who ushered Lady Sarah from the room and closed the door.

'She seemed a little frightened,' Captain Dufour observed, still writing his notes.

'We are all a little frightened,' Mary replied. 'We face the prospect of separation and imprisonment, with no idea of how long it may last, or of the conditions in which we are likely to be kept, and I believe that civilian prisoners are seldom exchanged.'

'Only if they have friends of sufficient importance to pull the right strings,' was the unsympathetic reply, but then he seemed to relent a fraction, and went on, 'Normally, internees are, one understands, lodged in ordinary town houses, and allowed a limited amount of movement within that town. You're not likely to be locked up in a cellar or kept in chains, or in a prison, unless you do something foolish. This may change, of course—the internment of enemy civilians is a new feature of warfare.'

'The last war went on for nine years,' Mary said. 'If this one lasts as long, Sir John would be past sixty when it ended, if he survived so long.'

'And you would be thirty,' was the cold reply. 'A shrivelled old maid. It's a pity we no longer have convents in France—you might have become a nun.'

'I'm a Protestant!' Mary said indignantly. 'And in any case, I've no wish to be a nun!'

The Captain looked at her, arrested in the middle of writing a word, with the result that his pen made a blot on the neatly-written page. He contemplated it for a moment, then sanded it, and patiently scraped it with a small knife from his inkstand until it had almost disappeared. Mary thought that the inkstand itself must be a source of annoyance to him, for it was a clumsy wooden thing, much disfigured with inkstains.

'No, I suppose not,' he said, finishing the sentence and signing his name. 'You have the appearance of a woman who should marry and have half a dozen children, not waste away in a damp cell.'

Mary sat in silence and considered the statement, wondering if it could possibly mean that he was inclining towards setting them free. Martin returned with Sir John before she had come to any conclusion—if, indeed, there was any conclusion to be drawn.

Sir John was remarkably subdued and made no protests at their detention, much to Mary's relief. He replied to Captain Dufour's greeting with equal courtesy, sat down, and then said diffidently. 'I've no wish to speak out of turn, but I must express a strong hope that you'll allow the ladies and Mr Brown to go on with their journey. My wife's health is not at all good, I'm afraid—she's been delicate ever since she miscarried some years ago, and she can't stand damp and cold. Mr Brown's health is poor, too, and quite genuinely so, for all he seems fussy and hypochondriacal.'

'And Mademoiselle Burns?' inquired the Captain in good English, with not very much of a French accent. 'What reason do you propose for including her with the others?' He had a little difficulty with the initial letter of 'her'.

Sir John gave Mary a self-conscious look, and replied, 'Well, she's young and pretty—ought to be finding a husband, not being shut up somewhere until maybe it's too late. It would be like caging a song-thrush!'

'Do you sing, Mademoiselle?' the Captain enquired coolly, still in English.

'Not notably,' she replied with equal coolness. 'Sir

John meant a wild bird, not necessarily one which can sing.'

'Of course,' the Captain wrote something on his fresh sheet of paper, and then continued in French, asking which political party Sir John supported.

'I suppose I'm a Tory,' he replied doubtfully. 'But I don't take a great deal of interest in politics, and I don't hold with wars. They're hard on country folk, and waste men's lives, people's money . . . I'm just an ordinary country squire, you know. I want only to tend my acres in peace and quiet.'

'Peace and quiet,' the Captain repeated in French, writing it down. 'Are you a magistrate?'

'Yes.' Sir John looked puzzled, as if he wondered what that had to do with anything, but Mary knew.

'Have you ever served in the Army or Navy?'

'Good heavens, no!' Sir John sounded as if he had been accused of suffering from some peculiarly noxious disease.

'You have a son?'

'No. We've no children, I'm sorry to say. The miscarriage I mentioned . . . first and last time m'wife er . . .' He cast an embarrassed glance at Mary, put out at having to mention such a thing in the presence of an unmarried lady. Mary reflected how little one really knew, even about one's best friends, for Lady Sarah's one pregnancy and its untimely end had never been spoken of in her hearing before.

'I'm sorry.' A polite expression of regret from the Captain, without apparent feeling behind it. 'What will happen to your estates when you die?'

'My wife will retain them for life, and then my brother's son has the reversion.'

'And how do your brother and his son occupy themselves?'

'M'brother's a clergyman, and the boy's at University.

Intends to enter the Church himself, I believe.'

Captain Dufour made a slight, non-committal sound, contemplated his sheet of paper for a moment, then rang his bell. As Martin entered, he rose unhurriedly to his feet and thanked Sir John, who perforce got up and left the room, looking distinctly puzzled, as if he was not at all sure what it had all been about. Once more, Martin closed the door and the Captain sat down.

'I'm sorry you don't sing,' he remarked, signing his notes on Sir John and sanding them.

'Well, I sing a little,' Mary admitted, 'and I play the pianoforte a little, too. Just as much as is expected of any lady.'

'You don't care for music?'

'Yes, but I like to hear it performed well, not in an amateurish fashion.'

After a brief silence, he said, 'Our blackbird is singing again—do you hear him?'

Mary looked towards the window, where the liquid notes could clearly be heard, and was momentarily over-whelmed by the recollection of what had passed in the garden the previous afternoon. By the time she had calmed herself, the servant had brought coffee and was serving it. The Captain stared straight in front of him while they drank it, and said nothing. Then he rang for Martin, and asked for Mr Brown.

After his usual greeting and invitation to sit, Captain Dufour returned to his writing and for a few minutes there was silence, broken only by the scratch of his pen. Mr Brown looked ill-at-ease from the start, and the wait caused his nervousness to increase. He fidgetted and cast one or two agitated glances at Mary, who was think-ing what a contrast the two men were to each other; the Englishman so fair and delicate in appearance, with such an expressive face, so impractical, living on a higher plane of beauty and poetry—albeit not of good quality—

far above mundane matters, whereas the Frenchman
was very dark and unexpressive in feature, apparently
extremely practical, yet with some hint of an appreci-
ation of natural beauty, and perhaps of music, creeping
through. He must have been a handsome man before he
was so cruelly disfigured, yet in a dark, saturnine fashion
—the beauty of the fallen Lucifer, perhaps, set against
the ethereal, slightly effeminate looks of Mr Brown.

'My apologies for keeping you waiting,' the Captain
suddenly said. Mr Brown and Mary both started, caught
unawares, and Mr Brown said, 'Oh dear! I mean—it's of
no consequence. I wasn't thinking of doing anything
else,' he added, with a gallant attempt at humour.

Captain Dufour regarded him with a total lack of
expression for a second, and then remarked, 'I trust you
are recovered from your indisposition.'

'Much better, thank you,' Mr Brown replied earnestly. 'It was only a cold in the head, of course, but I have to
take precautions lest it spread to the lungs. I have a sad
liability to infections in that area.'

'You mean that you take cold easily?'

'Rather more than that,' Mr Brown sounded the
merest trifle huffy. 'I suffered a severe inflammation of
the lungs as a child, and must beware of a pneumonic
attack. That's why I decided to winter at Cannes, for the
cold and damp of the English winter are most injurious
to me.'

Captain Dufour apparently wrote this down, hesitat-
ing momentarily over one word, and Mary, unobtrusively craning her neck a little to read what he had
written, made out that word was 'pneumonique'.

'It would, of course, make me quite unfit for service
with the Army or Navy,' Mr Brown added a little too
hastily, but this was probably due to his nervousness.
'Quite apart from the fact that I abhor violence in any
form.'

The Captain lifted his pen in mid-word to look at him again, rather as if he were an interesting specimen of beetle, and asked, 'Would you not defend your home if it should be attacked, then?'

'Well, in the unlikely event . . . well, no, I suppose not, for I don't quite see how . . .' Mr Brown floundered.

'And you would stand by helplessly while foreign soldiers raped your wife and murdered your children?' continued the Captain in a gentle, conversational tone. Mr Brown cast an embarrassed glance at Mary at his unfortunate choice of words, and stammered inconclusively to the general effect that he could not think what else he would be able to do in such circumstances, and then added, with a touch more spirit, 'In any case, I'm not married!' The Captain's eyebrows rose a little in pained astonishment, but he wrote down the gist of the answer, then sighed, put down his pen, propped his chin in his hand, and stared at or through Mr Brown in silence for some time, while the poor man coloured, then turned pale, and tried not to fidget, unconsciously winding and unwinding his handkerchief between his fingers.

'I do believe he's doing it on purpose, to make him suffer!' Mary thought. *'Well, I suppose that's better than shooting him or locking him in a dark cellar, but nevertheless . . .'* and she said aloud 'Have you any more questions for Mr Brown?'

Captain Dufour transferred his cold gaze to Mary, and the muscle by his mouth twitched once, as if to acknowledge his awareness that she realised what he had been doing.

'Is there anything that you think I should ask him?' he countered.

'You might ask what the effect on his health would be if he were locked up in your fortress at Sedan for nine years or so.'

'That would probably frighten him into a fit!' was the ironic reply. 'Surely you wouldn't wish me to be so cruel? No, I think I have no more questions for Mr Brown at the moment. Tell him, if you please, that he may leave us.'

When Mr Brown had gone, Mary said reprovingly, 'I suppose you think him a very ineffectual man, but there was no need to make fun of him!'

'Did I appear to do so?' Captain Dufour sounded mildly surprised. 'Well, perhaps a little. I hope you were not thinking of marrying him—I've no doubt he's very eligible, but a little too milk and water for you—besides, he admits that he would make no attempt to save you from the fate reputably worse than death!'

'That is absence from those we love!' Mary replied with icy dignity, for she knew her Cowper. Otherwise, she swallowed her indignation at the Captain's comment, for she had to admit that she had secretly come to the same conclusion. After another pause, she asked diffidently if the Captain had come to any decision.

'I shall inform you of my decision when I'm ready to do so,' he replied distantly. 'Meanwhile, I'm most grateful to you for your assistance, and I think I need not detain you any longer.'

CHAPTER
FIVE

Mary found her friends in a depressed state of mind when she rejoined them in the little parlour.

'I don't know how you could continue in that man's company for a whole morning!' exclaimed Sir John. 'A cold, unfeeling wretch as ever I've had the misfortune to encounter! He seemed to have a perverse intention of misinterpreting everything I said!'

Mary could only recall one thing which the Captain had misinterpreted in Sir John's interview, but she had no wish to seem to defend their enemy, so she kept silent. In any case, Mr Brown followed before she could speak with an anxious, 'Goodness only knows what impression he formed of me! I found most of his questions unanswerable! How can I tell what I should do in hypothetical circumstances such as would be totally outside my experience? I've no doubt he thinks I'm an arrant coward and a snivelling milksop, but that cold, glassy eye fixed on one so is enough to addle one's wits! I declare, I've never known any man make me so nervous simply by looking at me and saying nothing!'

'The most dreadful thing about him is that he is so correct and courteous, and so utterly enigmatic!' Lady Sarah took up the tale. 'I'm certain he hasn't an atom of human feeling—he's made of solid ice, all through! I dare say he has no idea of pity whatsoever, and I tremble to think what will become of us, at the mercy of such a—a monster!'

She dabbed her eyes with a minute handkerchief, and plied her vinaigrette as if her life depended on it.

'Has he given you no hint, no indication at all?' Sir John asked Mary almost pleadingly.

'None at all,' she replied sadly. She pondered whether she should tell them something of his history, but, while it might allow them to understand a little why he appeared so inimicable, it would certainly show them that they had excellent reason for fearing his hatred of the English, so she decided it would be better to leave them in ignorance.

Lunch was a decidedly gloomy meal, not improved by the arrival of an Italian couple seeking to return home from Baden to the Italian Republic, but in some difficulty because the wife had given birth to a child in Freiburg-im-Breisgau, which did not appear on their original papers, and the mother seemed almost hysterically convinced that the child would be taken from her. She had a piercing voice, which was frequently raised in lamentation at the imminent loss of her bambino. After nearly an hour of it, all four of the English friends decided to spend the afternoon resting in their own rooms.

Mary went upstairs with the others, and spent a little time going through her trunks to see what needed washing or mending, and then thought that it would be pleasant to sit in the garden. She took her sketchbook and pencil, crept downstairs, and scurried along the passage. As she passed the Captain's office, she heard the Italian woman's voice raised in impassioned speech, but had not enough Italian to understand what she was saying.

It was very pleasant in the garden. She sat on the edge of the fountain basin for a while, dabbling her fingers in the water and watching the fish, and then she walked along the paths, looking at the shrubs and flowers.

As she passed the Captain's window, she glanced in and saw that he was at his desk, writing, and appeared to be alone, but she did not linger in case he turned round and saw her.

When she reached the low wall between the garden and the cooper's yard, she saw that a small summer-house had been built in the angle between it and the town wall. It was almost unnoticeable from a distance because it was covered with honeysuckle, which she found to be a disadvantage when she looked into it with a view to sitting there. The interior was very dark and smelled damp and distinctly earwiggy, so she turned away and followed the path along the foot of the town wall. Halfway along to the steps, she came upon an alcove which contained a wooden bench which looked well-scrubbed, so she settled there and began to sketch the fountain against a background of dark shrubs and the prim, shuttered windows of the rooms of the inn which were beyond the garden door.

The sun was shining warmly, the blackbird was foraging in a nearby flowerbed, and the air was full of the humming of bees and the scent of grass and flowers. Mary drowsed a little between desultory additions to her drawing, until she heard the squeak of the garden door hinges, and looked up to see the Captain crossing the grass towards her.

He came to a halt in front of her and said, 'You make a pretty picture,' which she found a little difficult to assimilate as it was said without any expression. She decided that he was referring to her sketching, and replied, 'I fear that my drawing is of the same class as my singing and playing,' at which he gave a little sigh and shifted his weight in an unobtrusive fashion which somehow drew her attention, although she was sure it was not intended to do so. He looked very tired, she thought, glancing at his face.

'Will you not sit down?' she invited, moving to the end of the seat. He thanked her and sat down at the other end, half-turned towards her, at the very proper distance of more than two feet.

'Were you able to help the Italian family?' she asked, genuinely concerned.

'To some extent. They had omitted to obtain a passport for the child before they left Baden, where the Italian consul would have issued one with no trouble. I should have sent them back to Baden for it, but it was a great deal easier to assume that the child was born in Soleure, and write a passport for it myself. If he ever becomes famous, the Helvetic Republic will be credited with his birthplace, but it will serve the Badeners right— they shouldn't be so lax over identity papers!' He sounded half irritated, half amused.

'The parents must have been very grateful.'

He shrugged. 'I suppose so. At least, the mother stopped shrieking at me in Italian. The silence was very restful.'

Mary smiled, but there was no answering flicker of expression from him, so her smile faded, and she looked away across the garden, feeling that once more she had come up against the stone wall surrounding him.

'I've been considering what to do with you,' he said suddenly. 'And I've decided to let you make the choice.'

'I?' Mary turned a startled gaze on him. 'What do you mean?'

'The matter is evenly balanced. On the one hand, you are all English, and therefore enemies of France, and should be interned. On the other hand, this is the Helvetic Republic, not France, and it doesn't appear likely that any one of you is likely to pursue an active part in the war. Consequently, whichever choice I make will be acceptable in Paris. You will no doubt consider that mercy should dictate to me that I release you, but it seems to me that if I do so, I shall forfeit a chance to revenge myself on your nation for what was done to me when the positions were reversed. Perhaps you would argue that it would be unethical to use my public position to extract my private revenge, but I would reply that I had a public position as a prisoner of war, which was used to my detriment in a manner even more unethical. Perhaps my desire for vengeance sounds melodramatic to you, but then, you have not been disfigured and maimed, so I would reply that you cannot know how it feels. In any case, the French are notoriously a vindictive nation.'

Mary made no reply, for she was too filled with apprehension to speak.

'Well, then,' he continued after a moment. 'To your choice. I will give your friends and their servants passes to leave here, and safe-conduct to the border in Bâle, on condition that you remain here, as my wife.'

'Your *wife*!' Mary exclaimed.

'Yes. I'm prepared to concede you an honourable offer, although I'll admit that I considered the position of mistress at first. As my wife, you will have the entrée to local society, of course, and an establishment suitable for your birth and breeding. I think that our positions in Society are acceptably compatible by English or French standards. I own an estate in the Gironde, which provides a comfortable income. You will be able to live in the style to which you are accustomed, at least, and in a more interesting fashion, I think.'

'And the alternative?' Mary asked hopelessly.

'Internment for all of you.' His voice was coldly detached, without the least hint of a threat, yet inexorable.

'Then I have no choice,' Mary replied. 'I must . . . I mean, I thank you for your offer of marriage, which I shall be . . .' she balked at 'happy' and, after a hesitation, substituted 'grateful to accept.'

He made one of his slight bows, and then remarked,

'There will be no difficulties over religion. Marriage is a civil contract here, as it is in France.'

'You are Catholic?'

'Huguenot,' he replied. 'My family have been Protestants for two centuries—secretly, of course, until the Revolution, because of the persecutions. Our position has been similar to that of Catholics in your country.'

'Yes,' Mary said vaguely. She felt a numb sense of unreality—surely this could not really be happening? Perhaps she would wake up in a minute and find it was all a particularly vivid dream. How could she possibly marry this cold, enigmatic man?

'What shall I tell the others?' she heard herself asking. 'I daren't tell them the truth—they'll never accept it!'

'You think they would insist on internment, rather than let you marry me? Hm . . . perhaps you are right. I must appear a great villain to all of you.' Mary gave him a frightened glance, which he saw and greeted with a sardonic lift of one eyebrow, but he continued without comment on it. 'You had best leave it to me, then. I've no compunction about lying, being so deep-sunk in villainy. However, let us not be over-hasty. You've not had time to consider the matter properly. Perhaps you would prefer to think it over and give me your final decision later? There is no hurry—you may take a few days to be certain, if you wish.'

Remembering the nervous, frightened state of her friends at lunch, and knowing that she could not possibly condemn them and herself to internment, Mary shook her head. 'To delay can only weaken my resolution, and it would make no difference,' she replied bleakly. 'I have no choice—you must see that!'

'You are certain?'

'Yes. Quite certain.'

'Very well, then. I shall wait upon you all after dinner this evening.' He stood up, and then added, in his most sarcastic tones, 'After all, the majority of young ladies in my country, and probably in yours, marry men who are as much strangers to them as I am to you. Marriage in our class of Society is a lottery at best. At least you will have a comfortable position and a reasonable social life here, and that will improve, if anything, when we return to France. The only thing you have to fear is my private treatment of you, which may not be as terrible as you expect, and you will suffer the loss of your friends and your country, but the war can't last for ever, so you'll regain those in time. Apart from our intimate dealings, what you will gain by the marriage will be infinitely better than the misery you would suffer in internment. I'm not entirely a cruel man, I think. Once my craving for vengeance is satisfied, I may even turn out quite a reasonable husband!'

He did not wait for a response, but got to his feet and made his painful way back to the house. Mary stared after him, hardly able to think about the content of what he had said, for his tone had filled her with confused fears and doubts.

'It serves you right!' she told herself bitterly. 'You would daydream about noble self-sacrifice, and all that nonsense, and now you have to face the truth about it! Well—see if your courage matches up to your imagination, then!'

With that brave speech to herself, she dissolved into tears and sobbed hopelessly for some time, and then dried her eyes and climbed the steps to the wall-walk, where she stood for a long time, staring unseeingly along the valley towards the mountains, where the road ran which her friends would soon take, while she remained here, worse than a prisoner. She hardly thought coherently at all as waves of hopeless despair swept over her and engulfed her mind.

Eventually, she gave herself a little shake, and

thought, 'After all, it may not be so bad! He can't really
beat me, or starve or torture me, because he has a
position to keep up, and people would know—wouldn't
they . . .? I thought calmly enough about marrying Mr
Brown, if he should ask me, without going into the
vapours! He said I would be able to go into Society here,
and I expect it's little different from a town at home. I'll
be able to make friends, for at least I can speak French
tolerably well, and I shall have to learn German. It must
be better than being shut up in prison somewhere for
years, not knowing how long I must remain there. I
except there'll be children, for I suppose he'll want
some—an heir, at least, for that estate in the Gironde.'
She had only the vaguest ideas about the getting and
bearing of children, but assumed that they were a
normal product of a marriage, and the thought of two or
three of her own was very comforting, so she lingered on
that thought amid the other far from comforting ideas
which Captain Dufour's reference to vengeance put into
her mind.

Once more, the Cathedral clock and its companion on
the other side of the town reminded her it was time to go
in. By then, she was reasonably composed, and a good
wash removed the more obvious traces of tears. She had
very little appetite at dinner, but managed to swallow
enough to avoid comment from the others. In any case,
they were in no condition to take much notice, for they
were all very quiet and uneasy, and too wrapped up in
their own pessimistic thoughts for conversation. The
only good thing about the meal—apart from the food,
which was of the usual satisfactory standard, but might
just as well have been gristle, sawdust and pond-slime
—was the absence of the Italians, who had already
left.

After dinner, Johann came in as the servants finished
clearing the table, and said, 'Your pardon, ladies and

gentlemen. Captain Dufour would like to speak with you. May I invite him to come in?'

Expectant and apprehensive glances passed between the Robbins and Mr Brown when Mary translated his question, and then Sir John said, 'Please desire him to ask the Captain to step in, m'dear.'

Captain Dufour was apparently waiting in the hall, for he came in almost as Johann went out. He declined Sir John's courteous offer of a chair and a glass of wine in his usual coldly polite manner, and said in English, 'I will be brief. I find no occasion to detain Sir John and Lady Sarah, or Mr Brown or your servants any longer. You will leave first thing in the morning, and I shall provide you with safe-conducts to Bâle. Miss Burns must remain here for the moment, as I am expecting another party of English people, none of whom speaks or understands French, so I shall require her services as an interpreter, as it appears that there is considerable confusion about their credentials.'

'But we can't go without Mary!' Lady Sarah exclaimed. 'She can't stay here alone! She hasn't a maid, or a chaperone!'

'She will be provided with a lady's maid of exemplary character,' was the firm reply. 'And arrangements will be made for her to travel with the party which I mentioned, for some of them will certainly be allowed to proceed. She will probably overtake you before you reach Hamburg, as no doubt you will not wish to hurry, in view of the delicate health of two of your number.' There was not the slightest hint of sarcasm in his voice, or of anything else, for that matter, but Mr Brown apparently saw some implication in the last part of the speech, for he flushed and looked both annoyed and embarrassed.

'I think we should prefer to remain here until Miss Burns may accompany us,' Sir John's underlip projected in a determined fashion.

'I regret that will not be possible. You will leave here in the morning, willingly or unwillingly. Unless, of course, you prefer internment?'

There was no possible answer to that. Sir John might have been inclined to bluster a little, but his wife turned so pale at the mere idea that he wisely refrained, and only ventured a mild, 'Oh, very well, but you'll understand, I hope, that we're worried. M'wife and I regard ourselves as *in loco parentis* to the young lady, and you can't expect us to be happy about the idea of going off and leaving her here . . .' He was in something of a dilemma, for if he said what he really meant, the Captain was bound to be offended.

'You have my word that Miss Burns will not be interned,' the Captain said without a flicker of expression. 'I assume that you accept that even a French officer is a gentleman?'

'Yes, of course.' Sir John looked discomfited at the ease with which his mind had been read.

'Miss Burns herself has said nothing,' the Captain continued, thereby turning all eyes on Mary, who felt herself colour up. 'I trust she does not intend to raise any objections?'

'No,' Mary replied wretchedly. 'I put my trust in your honour as an officer and a gentleman, and . . . and I accept that I must remain for a time. I'm sure it will be all right.' She spoke in what she hoped was a confident and reassuring tone. 'I expect I shall be back with you quite soon.' Her eyes turned to the Captain's face, unconsciously seeking help and reinforcement, and he gave her a tiny nod which seemed to imply approval, and made her feel oddly comforted.

The next twelve hours or so were dreadful. After the Captain left them, Lady Sarah wept and Sir John fulminated, and Mr Brown fairly wailed his horror and distress. Mary was sorely tempted to tell them the truth, but

she knew that such weakness could only bring disaster
for them all, so she stood firm and interjected a reassuring, if mendacious, remark whenever she could.

At last, they exhausted their indignation at the Captain's stony-hearted villainy and went to bed, where
Mary lay awake, crying and praying, for hours, manag-
ing only a very brief and broken sleep, plagued by unpleasant dreams and not in the least refreshing. She got
up in the morning with the headache, and went, heavy-
eyed and listless, to the parlour for breakfast, where she
had to endure another chorus of distress and impotent
anger from her friends, until Sergeant Girard came in
and handed the bundle of passports to Sir John, adding
to them the single sheet of paper which was their key to
freedom.

'If you please, mam'selle,' he said to Mary. 'The bag-
gage is being brought down and loaded, and the coaches
will be ready to leave in twenty minutes.'

Mary passed this information on almost thankfully,
and the remaining time was taken up with tears from the
ladies and promises from Sir John to wait in Hamburg
for her, to which she managed to reply with a reasonable
sounding assurance that she was gratified by the
thought, but sure that there was no need, and she would
much prefer to know that they were going home as
quickly as possible.

She was saved from the strain of an emotional parting
by the appearance of Captain Dufour, who had apparently just recollected that he should warn Sir John not to
attempt to pass through Hanover.

'A French army is in occupation of the whole
country, and I believe that the Hanoverians will have
laid down their arms by now,' he said. 'On the other
hand, our commander is General Mortier, so I suppose
you could apply to him for a safe-conduct.'

Sir John gave him a look of intense dislike, and

hastened to get his companions into the coach in order to rid himself of the obnoxious presence. This had the advantage of preventing a protracted scene of farewell, which Mary would have found particularly agonising and difficult to sustain. As it was, she suddenly found herself staring at the archway through which her friends had vanished, and already the guard was closing the gates after them.

She began to shiver uncontrollably, and was only half aware of an arm about her shoulders which gently propelled her back indoors and into the parlour. She was pushed down on to a wooden settle by the fireplace and a firm hand guided her head to a resting-place against a shoulder covered in dark blue broadcloth. A silver button went in and out of focus a couple of inches from her eyes for a few moments, and then she turned away from it to hide her face, and wept quietly.

Some little while later, a quiet voice said, 'Drink this,' and as she lifted her head, a glass appeared under her nose. She took a sip, choked on the neat brandy, then managed a few more sips, and sat up, realising with confusion that she had actually been crying on the shoulder of the Enemy.

'Thank you,' she said, sounding dignified but woebegone. 'I think I shall lie down for a while, if you'll excuse me.' She put down the glass on the nearest table as she passed, and went upstairs without so much as looking at the Captain, for fear she should break down again.

Once in her room, she sat staring bleakly out of the window at nothing for a time, and then was disturbed by someone scratching at the door, to which she answered 'Come in!' in English.

The scratcher proved to be a short, plump, fair-haired woman of thirty or so in a sober blue stuff gown. Her hair was braided round her head in the old Swiss style, and she walked and stood in a curious manner, head thrust forward and tilted back, as if she were forever in a hurry, and always condemned to speak only to people much taller than herself. She had a round face, blue-grey eyes, and a particularly serene smile.

'I am Irma,' she said in careful, halting French. 'I am coming to be your maid, *ja*?'

Mary took an immediate liking to her, and rapidly discovered that she had a warm and understanding nature. They talked for a little while, and Irma explained that she was married, but her husband was away in the army, serving with the Swiss Brigade of the French Army. 'The Herr Captain says that he's forcing you to marry him against your will! What a droll humour! He says it so solemnly, one could almost believe him! He says you are to be married tomorrow, and you need a maid. He sent me to ask if I would do. I was a lady's maid before I married my Franz.'

'Oh, yes! I'm sure you'll do very well!' Mary replied thankfully, relieved that she would at least have one person she could like near to hand. Her mind was trying to assimilate the shock of the 'tomorrow'. So soon? Perhaps it was as well—at least she would have less time to worry about what was in store for her.

'We move all your things today, *ja*?' Irma was asking.

'Move?' Mary queried.

'To your new room. This is not a room for a married lady!' Irma's serene smile broadened to a happy grin as she nodded towards the narrow bed, and Mary realised that she thought the marriage was a love-match, having been completely misled by the Captain's sardonic manner. Very romantic it must sound—the dashing Army officer and the English lady, finding love amid the turmoil of war! Such a suitable story for a romantic novel!

Mary and Irma spent the rest of the morning sorting out Mary's belongings and repacking her trunks, for Irma insisted in taking everything out, shaking every garment, looking to see what it was, then carefully re-folding it. She was intrigued by Mary's English books, for she said she had never seen English written down in print before, and this gave Mary the idea of asking her if she would teach her German, which delighted Irma immensely. Then Mary went to the parlour and Irma to the kitchen for lunch, while the trunks were being moved by two of Sergeant Girard's men to her new room.

When she arrived at the parlour, however, Mary was redirected by Johann to the Captain's dining-room, where she found the Captain waiting. He greeted her formally and enquired if she thought Irma would be suitable for the position of her maid, to which she replied cautiously that she thought she would do very well.

'Don't feel obliged to take her if you don't really like her,' he said, serving her with a generous helping of cold chicken and salad.

'I do like her,' Mary replied, and tried to eat the food, but she could only manage a little, for it seemed like to choke her, with the dry, tight feeling in her throat caused by so much crying and the apprehension about her future which nagged ceaselessly in the back of her mind.

There was no further conversation. The Captain ate an abstemious meal, followed by two cups of coffee, then excused himself, saying that he wished to finish tomorrow's work as well as today's, as far as possible.

'Have you seen your new room?' he asked, pausing in the doorway.

'No.'

'You'll find it up the stairs by the garden door, just along here. The door facing the head of the stairs.'

After he had gone, Mary sat crumbling a bread roll for a while, and then collected together the crumbs, concentrating as though her life depended on not missing any, and went over to the open window, where she scattered the bread across the garden path for the blackbird. He flew down for them as if he was used to finding food there, and set to work with his bright yellow beak, keeping one beady black eye on her.

Presently, she sighed, and trailed upstairs in a dispirited fashion, and found her new room, where Irma was already putting away her clothes.

It was at the back of the inn, of course, with three long windows which overlooked the garden and made it far more bright and sunny than the old one. Its walls were painted white, and most of the floor was covered by a flowered carpet, which looked new, with polished boards round the edge. A large white tiled stove filled one corner, but the room was quite large enough to accommodate it, and several pieces of dainty satinwood or walnut furniture as well, without seeming cluttered. There were two or three chairs, a cheval mirror with a carved stand, a rectangular dressing-table with a dozen small drawers, and a mirror stand on top, and a matching wash-stand with a creamy marble surface and a bowl and ewer and various pots in a pretty turquoise blue, with sprigs of flowers and little birds painted in natural colours on white panels edged with gold leaves. Mary turned up one of the pots, and recognised the Sevres mark underneath with some surprise—surely not the usual furnishing of an inn bedroom?

The most dominating feature of the room was the bed. It was large and hung with pretty faded chintz curtains, matching those at the windows. Mary regarded it sidelong from various angles, and worried about its significance, for, like most young ladies of her time, she had only the vaguest idea of what was likely to happen in it, and the sight of it, occupying nearly a tenth of the room, and far larger than anything else there, filled her with apprehension, fear of the unknown.

Opposite the bed was a door in the wall. Thinking it

was a closet, Mary opened it and found herself looking
into a room about half the size of her own, with a plain
dark tallboy and dark-panelled closet doors on either
side of a narrow wooden bed. A soldier was brushing a
uniform coat on the slide of the tallboy, and he looked
round in surprise at Mary's incursion, and bowed like
valet instead of saluting when she hastily apologised and
withdrew.

'That's the Herr Captain's room, that is,' Irma said
over an armful of dresses and wraps. 'The closet is here,
behind the bed,' and indeed it was, obviously enough,
although the door was made to look like part of the wall,
with a small crystal knob to open it by.

Mary sat down at the dressing-table, which had its
own chintz-covered stool, and began to arrange her
small treasures in the drawers. She had not many—just a
set of silver-backed brushes and mirror which had been
her mother's, a string of pearls with eardrops and comb
to match, a garnet necklace, a coral set, and a crystal
bottle of jasmine perfume which she had purchased at
Grasse.

There was a curious thumping sound outside, followed by a rap at the door. When Irma opened it,
Sergeant Girard appeared with a casket held carefully
between his large hands. It measured perhaps a foot by
eight inches, and clearly matched the set of porcelain on
the washstand.

'This was meant to come up with the other,
mam'selle,' he said. 'What the Captain purchased yesterday, but the man at the shop forgot it, and he's just
brought it round now, with his apologies. And the Captain says you'd probably like to have some bookshelves,
so we've brought a set along from one of the other
rooms.'

Mary thanked him, and took the casket, to his obvious
relief. She put it on the dressing-table and admired it

while the soldiers carried in a small open bookcase and
set it against the wall between two of the windows. The
casket had a lock set in its ormolu mount but it was not
fastened, and when she opened it, she found that it was
lined with turquoise silk, with a matching velvet tray, in
which reposed the key, two gold slave bangles and a
folded note.

When the soldiers had gone, after some coming to
attention and saluting, Mary opened the note. It said
'For my victim/bride, Armand Dufour.' Mary was uncertain whether to laugh or cry.

'What shall you wear tomorrow?' Irma asked.

This was something Mary had not considered, and she
was not at all sure what would be suitable for a civil
marriage ceremony, so she asked Irma, who sorted
through the closet and produced one of Mary's favourite
gowns, a cream silk with a narrow bodice, pleated skirt
and little puff sleeves, embroidered round the hem and
neckline with flowers in a milky coffee shade. The back
fell gracefully into a short train, and she had an embroidered silk shawl to match.

'Yes, that will do very well,' she said. 'But what should
I wear on my head?'

'Most ladies wear a few flowers pinned in their hair, or
a piece of lace,' Irma said doubtfully. 'But it doesn't
matter, really. Your hair is pretty enough without trimming.' Mary gave a little sigh—after all, it hardly mat-
tered what she wore—the Captain was not likely to care!

Later, she dined alone with him in a curiously mixed
state of mind, half resignation and half repugnance. He
was as coldly polite as ever, and remained silent most of
the time, but he did enquire if she was sure that Irma
would be satisfactory as a maid.

'Yes, thank you,' Mary replied. 'She seems very capable and pleasant. Thank you for finding her, and I must
also thank you for allowing me such a pleasant room,

and for—for your gift . . . I'm afraid I haven't anything for you.'

'It would hardly be appropriate if you had, under the circumstances,' he replied. 'I trust that Irma informed you that the ceremony, such as it is, will take place tomorrow afternoon?'

'Y—yes,' Mary stammered. 'Where will it be?'

'At the Rathaus. I would have preferred a private affair, here, but General Eppler and his wife, and a few of my brother-officers wish to attend. I trust you will not weep too copiously!'

'*Odious* man!' Mary thought indignantly, and resolved not to weep at all, which was probably, she realised much later, why he had said it.

'There will be a semi-formal dinner here afterwards, for the same people. I've left the menu to Johann, but I'm sure he would be pleased to discuss it with you. Pray make any alterations you wish—you will, after all, be mistress of our household in future.'

There was a lengthy silence, and Mary began timidly 'Captain Dufour . . .'

'My name is Armand.'

She hesitated. To use his Christian name would imply an intimacy which she was not yet ready to accept, but she made a considerable effort, and continued, 'Armand, is there any means by which I may send a letter to my friends? They'll be worried if they hear nothing from me.'

'There's no particular haste, I think, as they're taking a circuitous route. Write whatever you think fit during the next two or three weeks, and I'll arrange for it to be sent to England in time for their arrival home.'

After dinner was finished, he suggested that they take coffee in his sitting-room, which was next door, between the dining-room and the little passage which gave access to the garden door. It was a plainly-furnished room, but quite comfortable, and well-provided with books, which filled two fair-sized bookcases. There was also a table in the middle of the room, with another shabby inkstand on it, and a pretty bonheur-du-jour between the two windows. An upholstered chair stood on either side of the fireplace, with a matching sofa a little to one side of the table. Mary sat in one of the chairs, with Armand in the other, and drank coffee. She tried hard to think of something to say, and received no help at all from Captain Dufour—Armand—who seemed able to sit in silence for long periods without any sign of strain. It was a relief when he roused himself from whatever he was thinking about to say, 'Pray retire whenever you wish.' She waited a few more minutes for courtesy's sake, then said 'Goodnight' and went up to her room, where she lay awake in the big bed, worrying and praying, most of the night.

The marriage ceremony was less of an ordeal than she expected. Her cream silk looked very well, although the face above it was quite pale, and the problem of her head-covering was solved by Irma producing half a dozen little cream roses, which looked well pinned to her chignon. When she went downstairs, Armand was waiting in the hall in full-dress uniform, looking a fine figure and quite handsome, in his sardonic fashion, despite his disfigurement. He looked her over with his usual lack of expression, and then said, 'Very beautiful, Marie,' almost as if he meant it. Sergeant Girard presented her with a posy of cream roses with coffee-coloured ribbon streamers 'From the Guard-room'.

There was a short drive to the Rathaus in an open carriage bedecked discreetly with a few flowers and knots of white ribbon, skirting round the Cathedral and drawing up before the fine Baroque doorway of the building, where a dozen or so officers and ladies were waiting. Armand presented them all to her; General

Eppler, a grizzled veteran, his pleasant, matronly wife,
The Mayor of Soleure and his wife, and French and
Swiss officers of various ranks, a few with wives and one
with a sister. They were all a little boisterous, teasing
Armand about his sudden embarkation into matrimony,
and apparently under the impression that it was a love-
match. Some of the remarks actually made him smile,
and this showed Mary why he normally did not do so—
the scars on his cheek made that side of his face almost
immovable, so that his smile was lop-sided, and she
realised that if he tried anything so broad as a grin, it
would look quite grotesque.

The actual ceremony was very brief. They were all
ushered into a large room, where the Mayor sat down
behind a large table, with Mary and Armand in two
armchairs facing him across it. Irma, who had come too,
took Mary's gloves and flowers and stood over by the
window, and the more important guests sat on velvet-
covered chairs behind the bride and groom, while the
rest stood about at the sides and back of the room. Mary
and Armand were requested to state their names, ages,
places of birth, and their willingness to be married to one
another. Armand gave the required information for
both of them—he had it written down, to save trouble
over the spelling of place-names, and all Mary had to say
was 'yes' when she was asked if she agreed to a contract
of marriage between herself and Armand. She managed
it without stammering or showing any sign of distress.

There were then some papers to sign, and Armand,
almost as an afterthought, produced a ring. Mary naturally began to extend her left hand to him as he turned to
her with it, obviously intending to put it on her finger,
and was quite surprised when he took her right hand
instead, pushed the ring over the knuckle of the third
finger (it was quite a tight fit) and then kissed her hand.
He then silently proffered another ring and his own right

hand, and she slid the gold band on to his finger with a sense of doom.

'Kiss your bride, sir, and that is all!' said the Mayor, who had conducted the ceremony in heavily German-accented French. Armand stood up and held out his hand to Mary, who rose and stood looking up at him, biting her lip to stop herself crying. He put his hands on her shoulders and kissed her lightly, with cool, dry lips, then turned away to receive the congratulations of his friends. Mary was left on a little island of desolation, only now beginning to realise that she was completely trapped, cut off from everything and everyone dear to her, and tied for life to this enigmatic stranger, who had already told her that he was marrying her for vengeance.

CHAPTER
SIX

THE return to the inn and the dinner-party passed in a
dream-like sequence of faces, laughter, compliments,
innuendoes, speeches, toasts. Mary somehow managed
to fix a semblance of a smile on her face, and murmured
the correct polite phrases, and, fortunately, Madame
Eppler decided that she was shy and discouraged the
others from making too determined an effort to draw her
into conversation.

And then, quite suddenly, they had all gone, and she
was alone in her bedroom, wearing only her nightshift
and brushing her hair like an automaton as she waited
for—for her *husband*!

She shivered as the word entered her mind, for this
was nothing like her past romantic dreams of marriage,
threw down the brush, stood up, and looked frantically
round the room for the escape which did not exist. There
were quite twenty candles burning in various candel-
abra, which seemed an extravagant number. All their
light seemed to concentrate on the bed, and she stared at
it, wide-eyed, on the verge of hysteria, until the click of
the doorlatch behind her made her spin round, and
Armand entered.

She stared at him in shocked surprise, for she had
never seen a naked man before, apart from a few
statues, and after one horrified look at what was tidied
away behind their fig-leaves, she blushed scarlet
and hurriedly lowered her gaze. Some curiously
detached part of her mind recorded calmly that his
lame leg showed the scar of the bullet-wound which had
crippled him, and the signs of the badly-aligned bones

at the seat of the fracture.

'That's something you'll have to get used to!' he said, sounding a little amused. 'And another is dispensing with this thing.' He flicked the lace trimming of her nightshift. 'I refuse to grope my way to you inside a bell-tent; I'll not take a—*a pig in a poke* I think you call it in England? Come, off with it!'

Mary gave a gasp of anguished horror and tried to back away, but he seized the garment and jerked it up over her head, stripping it from her roughly, and then rolled it into an untidy bundle and tossed it across the room.

Mary's hands flew to cover herself, but he caught her wrists and forced her arms to her sides, and she had perforce to stand there, stark naked, while he looked her over, much as if she was a work of art which he was considering purchasing. She closed her eyes, unable to endure the coldly impersonal way in which he surveyed her body. He even walked round to inspect the back view, and then remarked judicially, 'A trifle small-breasted for my taste, but you'll do very well otherwise.'

He moved away to the bed and flung back the covers.

'Come then!' he said impatiently. Mary made her hesitant way towards him shaking with fright, and lay on her back as he directed her, still in that curt, hard tone. She had very little idea what lay behind that little row of stars which novel-writers used to draw a decent veil over the secrets of the marriage-bed, and would undoubtedly have been utterly terrified if she had known. As it was, she lay there, cringing, in the pool of candle-light while Armand stretched himself out beside her in a leisurely fashion, leaning on one elbow.

By the time he touched her, she was too afraid to realise that the hands which explored her body were quite gentle, and when some hundred and sixty odd pounds of bone and lean, hard muscle crushed down on

her, she gave way to hysteria and tried unavailingly to
struggle. There followed a nightmare of panic, humili-
ation and pain, for she naturally tensed every muscle in
her body against him until he forced her into submission.

Then suddenly, it was over. She turned on her side,
drawing her knees up to her chin and crossing her arms
over them as she sobbed, too wretched to be aware that
Armand was standing at one of the windows, staring
sightlessly out over the dark garden and murmuring
something under his breath.

After some time, he turned back into the room and
went round pinching out the candles, then returned to
the bed, pulled the covers over her, and slid in beside
her.

'Marie,' he said, putting a hand on her shoulder and
shaking her a little. Her only response was another sob,
but he persisted, pulling and pushing at her body, quite
gently, until he had her straightened out, and then he
shook her again, and said in English, 'Are you listening
to me?'

'Yes,' she replied wearily, 'I'm listening.' His voice
seemed to come from some distance away, but she remembered afterwards what he had said, even if it meant
nothing at the time. She even recalled that he had
spoken in English.

'I think I was mad, but that's over now. It will never be
like that again, I give you my word. You must try not to
fight me in future, for it only makes things worse for you.
Better to relax, and try to think of something else, as
many women do. You may find, in time, that you even
begin to enjoy it!'

Mary gave another sob at the sheer unlikelihood of
that, but he went on, 'Now, you must accustom yourself
to sharing your bed with me, but I'll not trouble you
again tonight, so you may safely go to sleep.'

That also seemed unlikely, but within minutes, the

accumulation of sleepless nights and violent emotion had their effect and she slept. When she woke, it was morning and she was alone.

She sat up and stared unseeingly across the room, wondering vaguely how she could endure the rest of her life as Armand's wife. Then Irma came in with a tray bearing a pretty cup of steaming chocolate. After a careful look at Mary's face, she put the tray down and went over to her, wrapping a bedrobe round her bare shoulders.

'Was it very bad, Gnädige Frau?' she asked soothingly. 'Never mind—it will get better!'

'How can it?' whispered Mary.

'Oh, but it does! I loved my Franz very much when we married, but I screamed and wept on our wedding-night, and thought I could never endure another, yet within a week, I was longing for bed-time almost from when I woke in the morning! It's the same for most women, I think. It's only terrible at first, particularly if you don't know what to expect. The Herr Captain is a good man, and he'll teach you to enjoy it. After all, it's natural, isn't it!'

'He hates me,' Mary said dully.

'Oh, Gnädige Frau! You think so now, but you'll soon learn better! Why, of course he loves you! He can't take his eyes off you!'

'Eye,' Mary corrected, still sounding lifeless. 'He watches me.'

She took little notice of Irma's comforting monologue as she drank her chocolate, washed and dressed, and went downstairs slowly, reluctantly, afraid to encounter Armand and see the gloating expression which there must be on his face. She broke her fast alone, for he was already at work in his office, and she did not see him until lunch, when he entered the dining-room as the servants were putting the dishes on the table.

'Good morning, Marie,' he said impersonally. 'You slept well, I think.'

She gave him a frightened look and murmured something vague, then kept her eyes on her plate until coffee was served at the end of the meal and the servants withdrew.

'You've not eaten much,' he observed in the same detached tone. 'I trust you don't intend to escape me by starving yourself to death?'

'Would you care for some coffee?' she asked suddenly.

'If you please. With arsenic rather than strychnine,' he replied sardonically, and nothing further was said.

Dinner that evening passed in much the same way, except that Mary made no reply at all to his two or three remarks, but sat silent, putting pieces of what might just as well have been sawdust into her mouth and forcing herself to chew and swallow them, while the long-case clock in the corner ticked away the minutes to bedtime and whatever fresh horrors lay in store for her.

Those minutes passed very quickly, and it seemed no time at all before she was lying in bed waiting for him to come. There were only four candles tonight, so she assumed that he had seen as much as he wished of her, and she had pulled the covers up to her chin, although she fully expected that he would throw them off again.

He did not, however, but pinched out the candles and slid in beside her in silence. She tensed, waiting for his attack, and then something quite extraordinary happened, for when his hands touched her and began to move gently over her skin, her mind remained a cringing, frightened ball inside her skull, but her body gradually relaxed, and then began to respond to his caresses in a very surprising manner, and when at last he lay still and quiet beside her and her mind began cautiously to uncoil, it seemed almost as if her body was some separate entity which felt fulfilled and contented in a way which she had never experienced before.

For nearly two weeks, she moved about the inn with this strange feeling of division within herself. She saw very little of Armand, for he seemed to have unending work to do during the day, supervising the men who manned the town gates, dealing with applications for passes and permits of various sorts, and writing lengthy reports, which went off to his superiors each week with the returning courier who had brought him orders, letters and newspapers from Paris. Only on Sundays did he not go to his office, but escorted her to church, where the service was Lutheran and in German which hardly seemed suitable for either of them, but apparently was the only Protestant form available. Mary noticed that none of the other French people in the town attended, and the only Swiss she knew were the Mayor and his wife, who bowed and smiled in a friendly fashion. Otherwise, the short drive to and from the small church passed in silence, and she was isolated from any human contact by the language barrier, and the feeling that Armand was at her elbow, observing whatever she did.

Every day, he took breakfast with her, if she was up early enough, and lunch and dinner, unless he had to go out, and sat with her, in the sitting-room in the evenings, writing or reading. He replied courteously to anything she said, and occasionally made some remark himself, but once she had answered, unless she then volunteered something, he fell silent again. When the clock struck ten, he would lay aside whatever he was doing and rise to his feet, to stand looking at her until she, too, stood up and went upstairs with him. To her amazement, after the second night, what followed no longer seemed frightening or even distasteful, but she passed through a brief period of confusion to the beginnings of actual enjoyment, so that when, during the second week, he was twice out at General Eppler's headquarters until late and returned too tired to do anything but sleep, she was quite disappointed. She said nothing to him about her changing feelings, for conversation between them did not become any easier, and in bed he said nothing at all, and she was still too confused and afraid of him to break the silence.

Her days were very long and dull. She tried at first to take an interest in the housekeeping arrangements, but found that these were managed in troika by Johann, the cook, and Sergeant Girard, and although they listened politely to her suggestions, they clearly did not welcome them or need them, so she gave up trying, apart from a weekly courtesy visit to the kitchen, which was always spotlessly clean, and found other ways of filling her time.

Each morning, she spent an hour with Irma, learning German, which was the maid's first language, and made very good progress, having a quick ear and a retentive memory, but Irma had her work to do, and Mary felt that it was not fair to detain her longer. After that, she would walk briskly about the garden for an hour or so, whatever the weather.

After lunch, she sat outside and sketched, if it was fine, until she ran out of paper, or did her embroidery in the sitting-room, until she finished her piece and had not enough silks left to start another, and she read her half-dozen books through again. Then an afternoon came when she had nothing to do at all but pace about the garden feeling restless and unhappy.

Whenever she passed the window of Armand's office, she automatically glanced in, rather as a mouse might look to see what the cat was doing, and he happened that afternoon to be alone, writing at his desk. With a sudden little spurt of courage, she decided to ask if she might read one of his books, and went forthwith to knock softly on the office door.

'*Entrez!*' he called.

She went in nervously, and caught a look of surprise on his face as he glanced up, then rose and exclaimed, 'Marie! This is an unexpected pleasure! Pray come in and sit down—the sofa is the least uncomfortable.'

She obediently seated herself on the edge of the sofa, and he came to join her at the other end of it, and sat looking at her enquiringly.

'I—I wondered if I might read one of your books—in the bookcases in the sitting-room,' she said. Her eyes flicked briefly over his face, and then came to rest on his hands, which were lying idly on his thighs. They were sinewy, like the rest of him, with long fingers, and short, clean, well-shaped nails, and she felt her body stir deep inside at the memory of what those hands could do to her. She hastily looked away and coloured.

'Certainly, if you can find anything of interest among them,' he said, eyeing her with a little frown of concentration, perhaps wondering why she was blushing.

'Thank you.' She fidgetted with the handle of her reticule, and then said in explanation, 'I've nothing else to do, you see.'

'I thought you spent much of your time drawing and sewing.'

'I've run out of paper and silks.'

'Why not buy more, then?'

'I haven't very much money.'

'Your pin money is in the top right-hand drawer of your dressing-table. Use that for small purchases, and ask the traders to send me the bill for larger ones—within reason, of course—although I think you're not extravagant in your tastes.'

'Oh!' exclaimed Mary, 'I didn't know—thank you!'

'Marie,' he said, sounding half-amused, half-anxious,

'you mustn't think me an ogre! I've treated you badly, and I'm sorry for it now, but that's over. I shan't beat you if you ask for something, nor shut you up in the cellar on bread and water.' Then, with a complete change of tone and subject, without even pausing for her to answer, 'Several of the officers' wives are enquiring if you're ready to receive callers yet. Shall I tell them that our honeymoon is over, and they may call on you?'

'Oh, that would be pleasant!' Mary replied, her face lighting up at the thought of someone to talk to, some contact with the outside world. 'But . . .' she was suddenly deflated. 'But they would expect me to return their calls.'

'You may have the carriage whenever I'm not using it—I'll tell you in the morning if I shall need it. In any case, in this small town, you may quite properly go out on foot, as long as your maid is with you.'

'You mean I may go out? Outside the inn?'

'Of course. You may go wherever you wish. There's a low phaeton in the coach-house which you may use if you care to go into the country. Sergeant Girard will provide you with horses and a driver when he can, but you must give him a day's notice so that he can fit it into his duty rosters. The soldiers are here to control the movements of civilians, not simply to be our servants.'

'I may go out of the town?' Mary exclaimed. 'But aren't you afraid that I'll . . .' she broke off, shocked at what she had been about to blurt out, but he finished for her, 'Run away? Were you thinking of doing so?' he sounded mildly interested.

'No, there'd be no point, would there? I've nowhere to go, and you have all my papers.'

'You may have them back, if you wish. I'd rather you stayed here by choice than by compulsion. Your papers are here, in the bottom left-hand drawer of my desk. It's not locked, and you may take them whenever you wish.'

He looked at her in his usual unreadable way for a
moment. 'You would have no difficulty in crossing the
border at Bâle.'

'I've no pass to go out of the town.'

'You don't really need one, but here you are, if you
prefer to have it.' He went to his desk, took a card from
one of the drawers, signed it, then returned to the sofa
and sat down as he handed her the pass. She looked at it
half-unbelievingly, then put it in her reticule.

'Thank you,' she said, and wondered if he was tired of
her and wanted her to run away, or even wished that she
would so that he could have the pleasure of bringing her
back again, but she dismissed this last thought out of
hand, without even considering why she did so.

'I've no wish for you to leave me,' he said, presumably
reading her thoughts.

There was a knock at the door and one of the soldiers
entered. He stopped on the threshold and apologised,
but Mary stood up and said that she must not take up any
more of Armand's time, and hastily went out. She sat for
a while in the sitting-room, puzzling over Armand's
strange, contradictory nature, concluded that he was
still as much of an enigma as ever, then, with a sudden
determination to try out her new freedom, summoned
Irma, put on her bonnet and shawl, and went with the
maid for a walk round the town. A quick look in the
drawer of the dressing-table, which she had not opened
before because she thought it was empty, revealed that
in fact it contained two neat paper-wrapped rolls of
silver coins. She took some to buy her paper and silks,
and returned to the inn an hour later with a length of
sprigged muslin and a bunch of flowers as well, looking
and feeling much less despondent.

As she reached the door of the inn, she met Armand
coming from the opposite direction. He was limping
very badly, and did not see her at first, and she had time

to notice how tired and strained he looked with the effort of walking before he realised that she was there, and the mask of reserve slipped back over his face.

At lunch, he enquired if she had found what she wanted in the shops, and she told him what she had bought, and made a few comments about the town, which she thought very pretty and quaint. This was really the nearest they had come to a normal conversation, and she was emboldened by it to say, 'I didn't see you in the town—had you been very far?'

'I walk round every day, at some time, and visit each gate. It encourages the men, and gives me some exercise,' he replied, but in a cold manner which discouraged any pursuit of the subject.

Despite this sudden end to the more relaxed atmosphere, Mary was so grateful for the change that she ventured to kiss his cheek that night in bed. Apart from a sudden stillness in him which lasted for a full second, it evoked no apparent response, yet she was quite glad she had done it. It was not until some time later that she realised it was his scarred cheek which she had kissed.

Life improved a great deal thereafter. Almost every day, one or two ladies would call to see her, or she would make calls herself, and there was the town to explore. It was a picturesque, clean, and very pleasant place, with statues and fountains in the cobbled squares, and tall individualistic houses with brightly-painted shutters and windowboxes full of flowers. The market was full of bustle and life, and there were bargains to be had in fabrics, fruit and flowers. The Cathedral was beautiful, and the clock-tower in the Hauptgasse intrigued her with its quaint automaton figures of Death, a Knight, and St Ursus.

Then there were drives in the country. Sergeant Girard could not spare a man every day, only once or twice a week, but when he could, Mary drove out along the road towards Bâle, or southwards towards Berne or Burgdorf, sometimes going only six or seven miles and stopping to sketch or pick flowers by the wayside, at other times going further to enjoy the countryside.

Armand did not offer to accompany her on these drives, perhaps because he was too busy, but once or twice he drove her himself on a Sunday afternoon, handling the ribbons with an easy competency which surprised her, as she had always understood from Sir John that tooling a light vehicle like a phaeton was far from easy. Even more surprising was his horse-riding ability, for he asked one Sunday if she could ride, and when she owned to a moderate ability, had a couple of mounts saddled, and took her off across-country on what amounted to nearly a steeple-chase. She was hard put to keep up with him, but managed it with a feeling of satisfaction, returning home pleasantly tired and feeling healthy. As expeditions, these excursions, in the carriage or on horse-back, were odd in that Armand hardly spoke a word the whole time, and Mary gave up trying to make conversation, deciding that his silence was not exactly unfriendly and need not make her uncomfortable.

Two or three evenings a week, they dined out with various military and civilian gentry, or had people to dine with them. Armand seemed to fit in well at these gatherings, not saying much, but clearly welcome, and frequently referred to when a discussion needed a sensible opinion, or an argument settled. He did not remain near Mary, yet she was conscious all the time of his presence, a dark figure in the background, and felt his eye on her, even when a glance in his direction showed her that he was not looking at her at all.

After the first week of her new freedom, she wrote her letter to Lady Sarah. It was very difficult, and after several attempts, she decided to make it quite brief, and eventually wrote, after the usual greetings; 'I except you will be very surprised, and perhaps upset, to hear that I shall not be returning to England, at least until the War ends, not because I am interned, but because I am married to Captain Dufour! I know that you had good cause to dislike him, under the circumstances in which we first made his acquaintance, but I assure you that he is, in reality, a kind and gentle man, and I am only unhappy in my separation from home and friends, especially you and Sir John. I long for the day when I may see you again and when you may learn for yourself how good a husband I have in Armand.'

After all, she thought, it was partially true, and might even become wholly so by the time the war was over!

When the letter was finished, she folded and addressed it, and set it aside until Armand joined her for lunch, and then she gave it to him, saying, 'You said I might send a letter to my friends, to explain.'

'You've not sealed it,' he commented, after a glance at the folded paper, which he had been about to put in his pocket.

'I thought you would wish to read it.'

'Not particularly. If you've told the truth, I've no wish to embarrass you by reading it in front of you. Or behind your back, for that matter. Seal it before you give it to me,' and he held it out to her.

'I don't mind if you read it,' she said.

'Thank you, but I prefer that you seal it. You'll find wax and a taper in the bonheur.'

'How will you send it?' Mary asked when the letter was sealed and passed over to him.

'Under cover to a contact in Baden. It will pass from there to a neutral country, and then on to England by normal post. You'd be surprised how much traffic passes in that way. Sergeant Girard's new boots were made in Northampton—I'm sure you know where that is!' and he almost smiled at the irony of it. Mary thought that he was quite human at times.

'Speaking of traffic,' he continued. 'We shall be leaving here the day after tomorrow and going to Genève for a few weeks.'

'Genève!' Mary exclaimed. 'But that's in France!'

'Since '98,' he replied. 'What has that to do with anything?'

'I—I don't wish to go!' Mary blurted out in a tense, shaking voice. To be informed so suddenly and without warning that she was to go into enemy territory had been a considerable shock.

'That's unfortunate. However, my duties require that I go there to attend a meeting of officers occupying similar posts to my own, at which we shall discuss various problems arising from our work. I naturally expect you to accompany me.'

'I see. *My* duties require it, I suppose!' Mary's nervousness found expression in an unfortunate sarcasm. 'I suppose my wishes have nothing to do with it! So much for your desire that I remain with you by choice rather than by compulsion!'

Armand sighed faintly and sat back in his chair, as if deliberately relaxing.

'I shan't carry you bound and gagged to the carriage, nor drive you before me at a pistol-point,' he said quietly. 'Unless there is some good reason why you should not accompany me, I expect you, as my wife, to appear with me at the various social functions which will enliven our stay in Genève. Why do you not wish to go?'

'It's—it's in France,' Mary replied, avoiding his eyes. She thought herself that she sounded rather silly.

'And you are now a Frenchwoman. Has it not occurred to you that I could be transferred to a French city at any time, or that eventually, when my term of service ends, we shall live in France?'

'I suppose I hadn't really thought about it,' Mary replied wretchedly. 'It was so sudden, that's all, and the way you said it . . .' She broke off.

'Yes?' He leaned forward, resting his hands and forearms on the edge of the dining-table and looking searchingly at her face over the china and cutlery.

'You didn't ask me if I'd go. You said "we shall go", like an order.' She waited apprehensively, expecting an outburst of anger, possibly, or more likely some cold, dispassionate putting in her place. Whoever heard of a wife objecting to her obedience being taken for granted!

She could hardly believe her ears when he replied, after a momentary pause, 'I'm sorry. I thought the prospect of a change would please you. There's considerably more society in Genève than in Soleure. You'll be able to meet my brother-officers and their wives and move among a more enlivening group of people than the worthy Swiss merchants or Madame Eppler's little circle. Also, it would please me if you accompanied me.'

'Please you?' Mary was puzzled.

For once, he looked a little out of countenance. 'It has occasioned some comment that I suddenly married a lady whom I might more obviously have interned, and after a remarkably brief courtship at that! It would certainly give rise to more comment, and put me to some slight embarrassment, if I were to appear in Genève without you. However, I offered you marriage as an alternative to imprisonment, not in addition. If you refuse to go to Genève with me . . .' He lifted his hands in a gesture of resignation and sat silent while Mary digested his words.

'I—I have a choice, then?' she asked uncertainly.

'But of course.'

She bit her lip, feeling a natural revulsion at the idea of being paraded for inspection before French people— Frenchwomen in particular—who would undoubtedly find fault with her and make sneering remarks about her appearance, her accent, her Englishness . . .

'Of course,' Armand suddenly resumed in a calm, reasonable tone, 'it may be that there's some pressing reason why you wish to remain in Soleure of which you prefer not to tell me. A lover, perhaps?'

Mary stared at him in shocked amazement. 'Oh, you must be joking! You don't really think . . .?'

'Not yet,' was the enigmatic reply. 'But you're a beautiful woman.' It was a simple statement, not a compliment, but Mary found it oddly pleasing.

'Are we to eat any lunch today?' Armand enquired after a brief pause, and Mary hastened to pass him the soup which was growing cold in its tureen.

The light meal was eaten in silence, and when they had finished, Armand excused himself, rose from the table and went towards the door. Mary, who had been thinking about his words, came to a sudden decision and got up so hurriedly that she knocked over her chair, making him turn back at the sudden clatter.

'Please . . .' she said. 'Wait just a moment!'

He took a step or two back across the room, looking slightly puzzled, and Mary went close to him, looking up into his face.

'Is it true, what you said?' she asked. 'Would it really put you in an embarrassing situation if I don't go?'

He gave a slight shrug. 'No doubt I shall survive.'

'Would—would you—would you like me to go with you?' she stammered, an odd little note of wistfulness creeping into her voice.

'I have no wish to make you do anything which will cause you distress . . .' he began formally, then changed it to, 'Yes, I should like you to go with me.'

'Then I will.' Somehow, Mary's hands had found their own way to his upper arms.

'You're sure?'

'Yes,' then, with a nervous little attempt at a joke, 'I wouldn't wish you to think that I consider my lover more important than my husband!'

'I'm sure you have too good a sense of proportion and propriety,' he replied with a return of his earlier near-amusement.

Being so close to him and having so nearly quarrelled with him had weakened Mary's defences. She looked longingly up into his face and her eyes filled with tears, blurring her vision so that she failed to see his sudden frown, which might equally have been an expression of irritation or concern. A tear spilled over and ran down her cheek. Armand brushed it away with one finger, and then abruptly gathered her into his arms and kissed her.

For one delirious moment, it seemed that the tender lover of the night-time had ousted his coldly self-contained daytime counterpart, and Mary's lonely heart warmed to him as her body responded to his lips and his caressing hands. Then there was a knock at the door, and Armand raised his head sharply, uttered a word which had no place in Mary's French vocabulary, and gently released her.

'Who is it?' he called.

'Girard, sir!' was the reply. 'Sorry to disturb your lunch, but the Mayor's been waiting some time . . .'

'I'm coming.' Armand looked at Mary, hesitated, then said, 'Thank you,' abruptly and left the room.

When he had gone, Mary was filled with revulsion at the thought of what she had committed herself to doing. It might have been easier if she had been used to moving in Society, but she had spent almost all her life in a small village, and her only experience of social gatherings was limited to the few weeks she had spent in Paris with the Robbins. The tea-parties and informal dances at Cannes hardly counted, and Armand had just indicated that the society available in Soleure was not in the same category as that of Genève.

Perplexed and unhappy, she went to her room, summoned Irma, and reviewed her wardrobe. There was no time to order any new clothes, and the refurbishing and packing of what she had occupied all her time until almost the moment of departure, so it seemed to her that she suddenly found herself returning along the road which she had travelled so recently, remembering the alternation of fear and optimism which had marked that journey.

The coach in which they travelled was a hired one, fairly new, but, Mary thought, of inferior design to Sir John's comfortable berline. It had a distressing tendency to sway when the team drawing it proceeded at anything faster than a walk, and several hours of this made her feel quite queasy. The motion also seemed to affect Irma, who sat quietly in the corner on the same side as Mary, and spoke only when addressed, and then very briefly. Her silence might also have been at least partly due to the presence of Armand, who read his way steadily through an accumulation of copies of *Le Moniteur*. His valet had elected to ride on the box with the driver.

After a couple of hours of almost unbroken silence, Mary grew tired of looking out of the window and worrying, and ventured to ask, 'Who will see to the issuing of passes while we're away?'

'A man was sent from Paris. He arrived yesterday,' Armand replied, looking up from his newspapers. 'I hope he manages to avoid being murdered before we return.'

'M—murdered?' exclaimed Mary, disconcerted by the contrast between Armand's dry, sardonic tone and what he had said.

'He knows everything and considers himself infallible,

and France superior to every other nation,' Armand
gave one of his slight shrugs. 'He'll not make himself
popular. The Swiss don't consider themselves inferior to
anyone.'

He resumed his reading, but a few minutes later, he
silently passed Mary half a dozen copies of *Le Moniteur*.
She read them for lack of anything else, but found them
very depressing as they were full of the pronouncements
of the First Consul and the preparations on the
Boulogne coast for the invasion of England.

They made an overnight stop at Avenches, and arrived in Genève late the following evening, after a
wretched journey, for the heat was intolerable in the
valley of Lac Léman. Mary thought that she would never
have believed it possible that a journey through such
beautiful countryside could be so depressing. She had
almost given way to tears when they passed the customs
post at Versoix and entered French territory, the official
on duty hardly bothering to look at the papers which
Armand handed to him.

'They kept us waiting more than a quarter of an hour
here when . . . last time,' she said, feeling that she must
either speak or choke.

'One advantage of being French,' Armand replied.
'Also, Vaud has now joined the Helvetic Confederation,
so virtually counts as part of France—from the French
point of view, not the Swiss, of course,' he added with a
glance at Irma, who was scowling. She sniffed, but said
nothing.

Rooms had been reserved for them at an inn near
the debouchment of the Rhône from the lake, and
supper was served as soon as they arrived, but Mary
felt too tired, dispirited and apprehensive to eat, and
went straight to bed, not even bothering to inspect the
rooms. She expected to lie awake all night, but in fact
was asleep when Armand joined her, and was only

vaguely aware of his arrival beside her.

When she woke in the morning, he had already left to report at the Governor's residence. Mary dressed, looking distastefully at the bedroom, which was small and dark compared with her room at Soleure. There was a very poky dressing-room for Armand, little more than a closet, opening on one side, and a combined sitting and dining-room on the other, but she had to go out into the corridor to reach it.

When she had breakfasted, Irma brought her a note from Armand in which he apologised for deserting her for the day and informed her that they were to dine with the Governor in the evening, and there would be dancing to follow. This disconcerted her, for in Soleure she had carefully avoided accepting any invitations which included dancing from some rather mixed feeling that it would be hurtful to Armand to mention them, or that it would seem to imply some criticism of him that he could not dance. All her feelings about Armand were so confused and contradictory that she was unsure what her motives really were in anything which concerned him.

There was no question about his intention to go to this dancing-party, however. He came back to the inn in good time to change, and then sought out Mary in the sitting-room, where she was waiting in a pretty blue silk gown, twisting her long gloves about in nervous apprehension.

'We've time for a glass of wine before we go,' he said, going to the side-table where a bottle and glasses were set out. He handed Mary a filled glass, then stood sipping his own and looking out of the window, which commanded a view of Lac Léman. 'What have you been doing today?' he asked politely.

'Nothing very much,' Mary replied. 'I walked by the lake with Irma and then looked at some shops this morning, and visited the cathedral this afternoon.'

Armand turned to face her. 'I'm sorry I had to leave you,' he said. 'You'll meet some other ladies this evening, and then you'll find it more interesting, having calls to make and invitations to go out . . .'

'From Frenchwomen,' Mary thought, but she managed a smile and drank her wine, which made her feel a little less anxious as they set off in a hired town-carriage for the Governor's residence.

At first, the evening was quite as bad as she had expected. She met a number of Armand's brother-officers, who were reasonably polite, but looked her over as if they wondered why Armand had married her, and their wives, who were either over-effusive or distinctly cool, and all of them quite openly inspected her hair arrangement, her complexion and her gown and clearly thought them inferior. She was painfully conscious of whispered comments and disparaging glances, and overheard, as she was meant to do, a number of remarks on her foreign accent, her unfashionable gown and her 'roast-beef' complexion. The latter annoyed her, as she was well aware that she had a clear, English type of skin which compared to advantage with the sallow faces of most of the French ladies.

After the first introductions were made, Armand was engaged in conversation by two or three old comrades and Mary was left standing at his elbow, in the chattering circle but not of it, feeling very forlorn and unhappy, and smiling until she thought her face would crack if she tried to change her expression.

Just as she thought that she could not stand there another moment, Armand turned to her, put his arm about her shoulders and drew her further into the circle, saying pleasantly, 'This talk of old times is dull for you, my dear—I'm sorry!' and to her relief, the other officers took the hint and changed the conversation to more general matters so that she could at least join in a little.

When dinner was announced, Armand gave her hand an encouraging squeeze before leaving her to collect his partner, but even that small gesture, which might have given her a little confidence, was spoiled by a lady in white muslin standing nearby who had noticed it and made a sneering comment to one of her friends, and Mary was left waiting for someone to take her into a meal which she was sure would choke her if she attempted to eat any of it.

'Madame Dufour?' a loud, rather harsh voice with a strong German accent enquired.

For a moment, Mary failed to connect the name with herself, which drew a mocking laugh from the lady in white muslin, and then she recollected and turned to the speaker. He was a tall man with chestnut curls, sentimental blue eyes and a noble profile, of which he was clearly well aware, for he managed to show it to advantage by looking side-long at her in a slightly diffident manner. She realised that he had been introduced to her earlier, for he stood out among the dark-blue-uniformed French officers like a peacock among crows. His uniform was bright green with an inordinate amount of gold-braided frogging and gilt buttons down the front of his short coat, which had a scarlet collar and cuffs, and elaborate gold Austrian knots on the sleeves, repeated on the thighs of his trousers.

'Friederich Spengler, Captain, Chevaulégers of the Helvetic Confederation,' he reminded her with a pleasant smile, and offered his arm to take her in to dinner.

The relief which Mary felt at having a Swiss partner at the table instead of a French one was so great that she could not help but regard the handsome hussar as a rescuer, and was disposed to find him a pleasant companion, which, in most respects, he proved to be. His loud voice and over-attentive manner hardly registered on her consciousness, and his habit of looking sideways

at her she mistook for diffidence, not suspecting him of
conceit about his profile. She conversed with him in
French, but occasionally ventured into her newly-
learned German when she could recall a suitable sentence. Captain Spengler greeted her attempts with
admiration which at any other time she would have
thought overdone, but on this occasion it was more than
welcome, and the intervals during which she must con-
verse with the elderly Major on her other side seemed
painfully long in contrast.

After dinner, the company repaired to a ballroom,
decorated in opulent French Baroque style, where a
small string orchestra awaited their pleasure. Mary
naturally returned to Armand, who found her a chair
and stood behind her, leaning against the wall to ease the
strain on his lame leg, which did not take kindly to
over-long standing.

'Dance as much as you please,' he said quietly. 'I
regret that I can't partner you, but I've no wish to be a
dog in the manger about it, so don't let it inhibit you.' He
used the English expression, and Mary wondered if
there was no equivalent in French.

She gave him a grateful smile and waited with some
trepidation to see if she would have any partners, half-
hoping that she would, rather than be left too obviously
by the wall, and half-afraid that someone would ask her
to stand up for a dance with which she was unfamiliar.

The first few dances were cotillions and contredanses,
which she could manage, and a couple of Armand's
friends invited her to join in them, but then, to her
horror, the orchestra struck up an unfamiliar lilting
three-beat rhythm which she had never heard before,
and the couples who took the floor with obvious pleasure
and animation actually faced one another, the men each
putting an arm about his partner's waist, and she realised
that this must be the shocking, indecent waltz which the

French were reputed to adore, but which no proper
Englishwoman ever danced. Even the First Consul was
said to disapprove of it, which was why she had not
encountered it in Paris.

Captain Spengler appeared before her, bowing and
uttering a formal invitation to stand up with him.

'I'm afraid I d—don't know how to dance this,' Mary
stammered, feeling her colour rising.

'Oh, but it's very easy!' Captain Spengler assured her,
and everyone else, for his powerful voice caused several
heads to turn to see who could possibly not know how to
waltz, and Mary turned appealingly to Armand, but he
obviously misunderstood and responded by gesturing
her on to the floor in an encouraging manner, so she had
to stand up and do the best she could, which resulted in a
clumsy and ungraceful performance, her feet seeming to
take on a perverse will of their own and her body stiffen-
ing of its own accord at the impropriety of dancing with
the arm of a strange man around her.

'You seem ill-at-ease, dear lady,' Captain Spengler
said in her ear. 'Pray, count me your friend and tell me
what troubles you.'

'Nothing at all,' Mary replied breathlessly.

'You're very brave, but I understand how distasteful
this gathering must be to you! I see it in your eyes, in the
tone of your voice! Oh, you smile, and thereby deceive
the undiscerning, but I see beyond the façade, and I
know you're unhappy! How may I serve you?'

'You're mistaken!' Mary tried to assure him, but
someone tittered as she stumbled in a mis-step and her
troubled expression gave the lie to her words. The look
of concern and sympathy in Captain Spengler's blue eyes
was a comfort she could not help but welcome. At least
there was one sympathetic and friendly person among all
these enemies!

The Swiss Captain danced with her twice more before

the evening ended, and those were the only dances she
could possibly be said to have enjoyed. She left the
Governor's house with relief, and sank into a dark corner of the carriage feeling utterly wretched at the
thought of having to go through a similiar ordeal over
and over again during the next few weeks.

'I gather that the waltz is not yet popular in England,'
Armand observed as the carriage moved off.

'No. It's not considered proper, I believe,' Mary
replied.

'You'll soon learn to do it well—you're light on your
feet, with a good sense of rhythm. No doubt your gallant
Swiss admirer will teach you.' Armand sounded faintly
amused.

'Oh. Do you mean Captain Spengler?' Mary asked
unhappily. 'I don't think he's an admirer—he was just
being kind.'

Armand made a slight sound which might have been a
snort of laughter or of disgust.

'He's a sentimental fool masquerading as a soldier—
never seen a shot fired in anger in his life, apart from a
few duels! His family owns a porcelain manufactory, I
believe, and he occupies his time in spending the large
income it provides, while peacocking about in that rid-
iculous uniform pretending to be a liaison officer between the French and Helvetic Armies! I don't mind if
you flirt with him a little, within reason, so don't feel
obliged to set him down!'

'I don't flirt,' Mary replied disconcerted.

'Why not? It passes the time, and everyone else does!'
Armand replied indifferently.

Mary was upset by this exchange, although the rest of
the evening passed as usual, and Armand made love to
her in his usual skilled and silent fashion when they went
to bed. She was still awake at dawn the next morning,
lying still for fear of disturbing him, and thinking dis-

jointedly about the stranger beside her, trying to examine her confused thoughts about him.

He still frightened her because he was so unreadable, and she felt that she knew almost nothing of what went on behind that mask which he set as a barrier between them, and yet she could not be content to leave him to his cold detachment. She was beginning to realise that, if she were honest with herself, she had grown fond of him, which seemed strange under the circumstances.

She carefully drew herself up in bed and, leaning on her elbow, took a long and searching look at his face, which was something she could never find the courage to do while he was awake. His eye-patch had come off and lay on the pillow by his head, almost lost among his dark curls.

She had been surprised at the marriage ceremony to hear him give his age as twenty-six, for normally he looked older, but now, with his face relaxed in sleep, he seemed to have shed several years. The taut look about his mouth had gone, and even the deep grooves which made his expression so saturnine seemed less pronounced. She noticed for the first time that his mouth was finely-chiselled and looked sensitive, not hard and thin-lipped as she had thought. He must have been a handsome man before . . .

Then she made herself study the left side of his face. One jagged scar ran vertically from an inch above his eyebrow to the corner of his mouth, gouged deep across the eye-socket, and the other crossed it at an acute angle, starting higher up, but more to the side of his brow, and ending almost at his nostril. It was hideous, but her principal reaction was to think how agonisingly painful it must have been, far worse than the pain he had caused her during that dreadful first night.

'I can hardly suppose that you're admiring your handsome husband!' he remarked coldly, and Mary realised that his eye was open and looking at her, and all the lines were back in his face. She was too confused to take in what expression, if any, was visible.

'I d—didn't mean—I thought you were asleep . . .' she said wretchedly. 'I'm sorry . . .'

'For what?'

'For what happened to you . . . for all you've suffered . . . for staring at you . . .' and her over-wrought nerves gave way and she dissolved into tears.

He said nothing at all, but sighed, and pulled her down into his arms, settling her head against his shoulder, and gently stroked her hair until presently she grew quiet and then drifted into sleep. When she woke, it was past nine and she was alone.

CHAPTER
SEVEN

MARY was surprised to receive, later that morning, several invitation-cards from ladies she had met at the Governor's party, and when she asked Armand what she should do about them, he said, with no great interest, 'Oh, do as you please. Accept whichever attracts you—don't refuse any from the Governor or a senior officer's wife, of course!'

As a result, Mary found herself going out somewhere most afternoons, on drives or picnics, or to conversation- or card-parties in the various salons which the ladies had contrived to establish in the inns in which they were staying, or in the houses of those who were resident in the city, and she ventured on one or two such gatherings herself, limited by the smallness of her sitting-room. Her evenings were occupied by dinners, dancing-parties and other entertainments to which Armand accompanied her. She wondered once or twice what Jean Calvin would have thought of such goings-on in his Godly City!

She wondered much more frequently why the ladies invited her, for they were no more friendly on closer acquaintance than they had seemed at first, and obviously took pleasure in putting her to the blush whenever they could contrive to do so. One conversation which started innocently enough about the many fine houses and estates along the shores of the lake was a typical example of the traps into which she found herself blundering. One lady remarked that the estates seemed quaintly informal in appearance, and Mary was dismayed to hear her own voice saying, 'No doubt their owners have gone to a great deal of trouble to arrange them so, for we do so at home . . .' she broke off, but too late.

'At home?' queried a honeyed voice. 'In Soleure, you mean?'

'In England,' Mary tried to speak steadily, but her voice betrayed her.

'You must be very anxious about your home,' remarked another honeyed voice, full of false sympathy. 'Of course, when England is added to the French domains, you will at least have the advantage of a French husband! So very far-sighted of you, and so sensible! Marriage, of any sort, must be preferable to imprisonment, or the discomfort of living in a conquered country!'

'No doubt,' Mary replied stiffly, and then attempted to force the conversation into a less painful channel. 'I believe that Madame de Staël owns one of those estates we were discussing. Is she resident there now, do you know? I should like very much to meet her.'

This obviously disconcerted all the half-dozen ladies present and caused quite a flutter, and then their hostess said in agitated tones, 'Oh, pray don't mention that person! She's incurred the displeasure of General Bonaparte—the First Consul, I should say—and is not received or recognised in Society *at all*!'

Mary felt quelled by their disapproval, but it occurred to her afterwards that at least she had managed to upset their smugly patronising attitude to herself, albeit accidentally. Another unexpected result of her *faux pas* came a day or two later, when Armand, having a few hours to spare, invited her for a drive along the lakeside. At one point, he nodded towards a house visible behind some trees and said, 'That's where M. Necker lives. Unfortunately, he's not at all well and doesn't receive visitors, and his daughter is from home at present, or I'd take you to visit her, despite the First Consul!'

'His daughter?' Mary queried.

'Madame de Staël,' Armand replied. He made no further comment on the subject, but went on immediately to something else, and Mary was left with an uncomfortable feeling that someone had reported her *faux pas* to him, probably with the intention of making trouble. She recognised with a certain ironic amusement that it was typical of Armand to react in any but the expected manner!

This daytime excursion with him was a rare exception to the usual pattern, as he was far too occupied with meetings during weekdays, but he accompanied her in the evenings, and these entertainments were far less of an ordeal, for Armand's brother-officers were less spiteful and unfriendly than their wives, and at least talked to her pleasantly and asked her to dance, although she realised that it was only to oblige Armand, who was properly attentive to her on these occasions, but seemed very preoccupied and silent when they were alone together. Mary tried to believe that his thoughts and energies were taken up by his daytime meetings and dicussions, but she could not help wondering if he regretted marrying her now that he saw how ill-suited she was to the social circles in which he expected her to move.

By the end of their first two weeks in Genève, she felt that the gulf between them was growing deeper and wider every day. He put on a good performance of husbandly devotion in public, which appreciably reduced the number of speculative looks and whispered comments, but in private he hardly spoke and seemed uninterested in her daytime occupations. At night, he made love to her less often, and she lay awake on several nights wondering if he was really tired or just pretending because he was bored with her.

Captain Spengler, on the other hand, seemed to take a genuine and growing pleasure in her company, and appeared at almost every function she attended, other than those which were exclusively feminine. Consequently, when the Governor gave another dancing-party towards the end of their third week in Genève, she was not particularly surprised to find herself standing up with Captain Spengler two or three times, but when he asked to take her out to supper, she hesitated and replied, 'I think perhaps my husband . . .'

'Your husband!' exclaimed Captain Spengler. 'Oh, no! See, he's sitting down to cards in the next room,' and through the open double doors, Armand was visible by one of the small tables, just propping his stick against a chair preparatory to seating himself, so Mary accepted Captain Spengler's invitation.

As she was in the middle of eating a confection of ice-cream, he suddenly leaned across the little table between them and said, in his idea of a low whisper, 'I cannot remain silent! I must speak! Dear lady, I am *appalled*!'

'I beg your pardon?' Mary looked at him in wide-eyed surprise, her spoon poised in mid-air.

'I can't imagine how you can bear to be married to Captain Dufour! No wonder I detect sorrow, behind your brave exterior! I find it quite horrifying that you should be tied to that man! Why, one has only to look at him to see that he's a monster!'

'Captain Spengler!' Mary exclaimed, trying to keep her voice down, for one or two people had glanced in their direction during his last outburst. 'You go too far! My husband may have suffered a misfortune, but he is *not* a monster!'

'Forgive me, dear lady! You mistake me—I do not refer to his disfigurement alone!' He shook his head and raised his hands in a gesture which seemed to indicate that he was lost for words, although in fact he continued at full spate. 'The strength of my sentiments carried me beyond the bounds . . . My deepest apologies! Oh, I admire you, dear lady! Your courage, your loyalty!'

'I would prefer that you do not continue this conversation!' Mary said with all the icy dignity she could muster. 'I wish to return to the dancing, I am engaged for the next dance,' and she pushed aside the rest of her ice, rose to her feet, and went, so that Captain Spengler had perforce to follow. Once they were back in the long room, she went straight to her next partner without a glance at Captain Spengler, and carefully avoided him for the rest of the evening.

On the way home, a little after midnight, Armand enquired coolly in the darkness of the carriage, 'Have you fallen out with your cavalier?'

'My . . . ? Whom do you mean?' Mary asked on a very false note of surprise.

'The handsome manufacturer of chamber-pots. You went out to supper with him, returned in a state of high dudgeon, and cut him dead the rest of the evening. Presumably you had a reason?'

'Yes. He was rude,' Mary replied firmly.

'To you?' The question cut through the darkness in a voice which sounded to Mary like a sharpened icicle.

'No.' She wished she could see his face. 'He said something about—about someone else which I thought was unkind and not true.'

'Should I call him out, or merely horsewhip him?' Armand said at his most sardonic.

'Neither, I think,' she replied calmly, having concluded several weeks before that this particular tone indicated that he was joking. 'I gave him a set-down, and he apologised.' It was partly true, if one overlooked the insinuation which had followed the apology.

'Ah well—I suppose being flung into outer darkness is

punishment enough, then. Presumably you'll forgive him eventually?'

'I don't know,' Mary replied uncertainly. 'I thought he was kind and a good friend, but he had no right to say such dreadful things . . .' She broke off, suddenly realising that her tongue was running away with her, and also that she had come to count on Captain Spengler's attentions and friendliness more than she had known.

Armand put his head out of the window and instructed the coachman to drive over the Rhône bridge and along the lake-side road for a while.

'You'd better tell me, I think,' he said to Mary in an enigmatic tone as he closed the window again.

'It was so unexpected,' she replied unwillingly. 'He's been kind and attentive, and he doesn't exactly flirt, so I thought he was just being pleasant because—well, because he saw how *un*pleasant some of the French ladies are . . .' She tailed off, not knowing how to continue.

'Also, he's a handsome, well-set-up man, and obviously admires you very much,' Armand observed in a neutral tone. 'Under the circumstances, you're bound to find him attractive. I'm sorry that the ladies have been unkind to you. I should have realised that it was likely to happen. They've too little to occupy their time, and fill it with gossip, like most females of their kind. Have they made you very wretched?'

Mary hesitated, and then replied evasively, 'I shall be glad to go home.'

'Home?' he asked sharply.

'To Soleure.' Strange to find that she actually thought of it as home now.

'It shouldn't be long now—another two weeks at the most. What did he say?' Armand suddenly pounced on what she had been trying to avoid.

Defeated, Mary shut her eyes and said very rapidly, 'He said he was appalled that I was married to you, and

couldn't imagine how I could bear it and he thought I
seemed sad behind my brave exterior, and he found it
horrifying that you should have married me and that
you're a monster,' and then stopped as suddenly as she
had started.

After a moment's silence, Armand said calmly, 'Is
that all?'

'Yes.'

'Somewhat tautological, but true enough,' Armand
observed. 'Unkind, I agree, but I can't imagine why you
thought it untrue. What was wrong with his apology?'

'He said he admired my loyalty,' Mary dissolved into
tears for no reason that she could have explained, even
to herself.

Armand said nothing, but moved across to the seat
beside her and took her in his arms.

'He's quite right about that,' he said gently. 'I appreciate your setting him down on my behalf, for it must have
been difficult for you to contradict him! Don't be too
hard on him, Marie—it sounds as if he may be genuinely
concerned about you, and you don't want to lose one of
the few friends you have here! Do you like him very
much?'

'I d—don't know,' Mary tried to answer as honestly as
she could. 'He's been very pleasant . . .'

'Never mind, then. I should think he'll be more careful what he says after this. Dry your tears, and we'll go
back to our lodging. I must confess that I'm very tired.'

It was the first admission of physical weakness he had
ever made to Mary, and she found it comforting, thinking that his apparent indifference since they came to
Genève must have been due to fatigue after all, and
certainly he was once again the gentle and considerate
lover that night, so that she felt almost grateful to Captain Spengler for this result of his outburst, although she
hoped very much that he would not repeat it. Surely she

had made it clear to him that she would not listen to such comments about Armand?

And so, for a few days, it seemed. Mary dined out, accompanied by Armand on two successive evenings when Captain Spengler was also among the guests. She was coolly polite to him, no more, and her occasional covert glances at Armand showed her that he gave the Swiss one or two quizzical looks, but otherwise took no more notice of him than usual. Captain Spengler behaved correctly, apart from a few anguished and pleading glances in her direction, and mostly stood about looking melancholy and thoughtful, and showing off his noble profile to advantage.

A week passed. Captain Spengler's outburst receded into history. Then came a very wet day, and Mary was seated by the half-open window of the sitting-room, doing her embroidery in a desultory fashion between watching the rain, and feeling a little lonely and depressed, when Captain Spengler strode into the room, unannounced, in the full glory of his green, gold and scarlet uniform, complete with plumed mirliton, sabretache and sabre.

'Oh, you surprised me!' Mary exclaimed, alarmed by the sudden incursion.

'I'm deeply sorry, but I could find no-one to announce me. Forgive me, dear lady!' he exclaimed. 'I could bear it no longer! I felt I must speak to you in private, and I felt sure that you'd have no other callers on such a day, so I took the liberty of coming to you!'

'How did you get in?' asked Mary.

'I told the guard at the gate that I was expected, and found no-one about in the building. May I sit down for a few minutes and tell you why I've come?'

Mary made a half-hearted gesture of assent. She had always found him an attractive man, despite his loud voice and over-emphatic mode of speech, and this made

her uneasy, for her life with Armand was difficult
enough without the added problem of becoming in any
way involved with another man. She wished he would
lower his voice, for it was far too loud and penetrating
for comfort, and could probably be heard outside the
room.

Captain Spengler put his mirliton with its red and
yellow plume carefully on the table and tossed aside his
cloak, which landed half across the back of a chair and
proceeded to drip on the polished floorboards in a melancholy fashion. Then he drew up a chair a good deal
closer to Mary than she liked, fixed her with a very
serious look, and began his explanation.

'I was most impressed by your loyal and very proper
reaction to my most improper outburst at the dance-
party, and yet puzzled that you refused to hear a word
against your—against the Captain. I've since made discreet enquiries—a little here, a little there—and I think I
begin to understand. You are English, I believe?'

Mary warily admitted that she was.

'Ah! And that Corsican bandit who rules France
ordered the internment of English travellers in France—
but it's not altogether clear if this applies in Switzerland
—I cannot adopt the stupid titles that man foists upon
us! It rests with the officials in the various towns and
cantons, French or Swiss, to decide? I see from your face
that I'm on the right lines! You arrived in Soleure with
three friends and some servants, and after three days,
they were allowed to go on their way, whilst you remained there, and the *very next day*, you *married Captain Dufour*! He happens to be the official who deals with
passports in that town! In other words, the *gallant* Captain forced you to marry him, for whatever reason, in
exchange for the freedom of your friends! No, you cannot deny it!' as Mary made a sound of protest.

'But I fail to see what business it is of yours that I . . .

My marriage is not your concern, Captain Spengler!'
Mary managed to get in, but only by raising her voice
above his, and without any effect, for he continued
without listening to her.

'I was indeed right in calling him a monster! Quite
apart from his disfigurement, which I admit he cannot
help, but which any right-thinking man would agree
must make it quite impossible for him to think of marriage—it might lead one to pity him, were he other than
he is, but, apart from that, as I say, he's a cold, sarcastic
creature, and, I dare swear, cruel into the bargain! To
force you into marriage with him in such a way! And I
believe he ill-treats you!'

'Indeed, no!' Mary cried vehemently, but without
effect.

'I've seen how he watches you! I've seen how you look
towards him before you dare do anything, afraid that his
frown may warn of unjust retribution to come! I cannot
bear to think of it! I must rescue you—it would be my
Christian duty, even if I were not your devoted admirer!
I beg you, dear lady, to trust me! Have no fear! This—
this *Frenchman* shall no longer tyrannise over you! I
shall protect you from him! Fly with me! Let me save you
from him!'

Staring at him in horrified consternation, Mary
thought quite clearly that he was being ridiculously
melodramatic—'Fly with me!' indeed!—but she was
momentarily incapable of speech, and he seemed to take
her silence for assent.

'I know you must fear that he'll prevent you, and take
some dreadful revenge on you for even thinking of
escape, but I promise you shall go far beyond his reach! I
have estates in Vaud, which is still independent, and in
Austria, where you will be safe from the machinations of
a trumpery infantry captain! Come with me, dear lady!
He forced you into marriage against your will, and an-

nulment in those circumstances will present no difficulties! I have everything planned!'

'Captain Spengler!' Mary found her voice and positively shouted him down. 'Stop it! Stop it at once! You're
mistaken! I will not listen!'

'But dear lady . . .'

Seeing there was nothing else to be done, Mary clap-
ped her hands over her ears and ran for the door,
wrenched it open, and flung herself out of the room. As
the slam of the door behind her reverberated through
the inn, she ran full tilt into the arms of Armand, who
was standing in the passage. He gave a slight grunt as he
received the full force of her impetuous charge, then
steadied her with his hands on her shoulders, and, without a word, half-pushed, half-pulled her into the bedroom, shut the door and turned the key in the lock.

Mary subsided into a chair with her hands over her
face, breathing hard and half-sobbing. She heard the
sitting-room door open again, and Captain Spengler,
sounding both puzzled and anxious, call softly, 'Madame? Madame Dufour? I beg you, dear lady . . .!' He
tried the bedroom door, then went back along the passage and called up the stairs. Eventually, receiving no
response, he apparently gave up, for he returned to the
sitting-room, presumably to collect his belongings, and
then his footsteps receded down the passage.

With a sigh, Mary relaxed and dropped her hands into
her lap.

'Why did you lock the door?' she asked inconsequen-
tially, not knowing what else to say.

'It'd have been damned awkward if he'd walked in
here,' Armand replied coolly, 'He'd have found me
standing over you with a good stout stick in my hand,
and I shudder to think what he'd have made of that! I'd
have been forced to a meeting with him, and I've no wish
for it!'

'Meeting?' Mary was not sure what he meant, but his brief reply, 'Over pistols,' enlightened her. 'D—did you hear what he said?' she asked nervously.

'I could hardly do otherwise! If he hasn't the sense to lower his voice when he attempts to seduce another man's wife, I wonder he isn't shot as full of holes as a colander by now! I happened to be changing my wet clothes in my dressing-room, when he arrived. The doors were open—not that they needed to be! I thought I'd best come in in case he tried to ravish you—no woman should be expected to put up with that twice in one year!'

'What shall you do?' Mary asked, relieved that he had heard everything, but anxious about his reaction.

Armand gave one of his brief almost-shrugs. 'It depends on what he does next. You've sent him to the rightabout—if he has the sense to accept that and go away, well and good—after all, he was quite right, and he meant well, up to a point—but if he persists, I suppose I shall have to take some notice of him. Unless you wish to run off with him, of course.'

Mary looked at him in blank astonishment, but could read nothing in his face.

'What do you mean?' she asked.

He drew up a chair and sat down facing her, very much as Captain Spengler had but not coming nearly so close, and said quietly, 'What he said was true, as far as it goes, you realise. From his point of view, he's made a reasonable proposition. It would be easy enough for you to go with him.'

'But you have my papers,' Mary pointed out.

'They're in the top drawer of the tall-boy there.' Armand indicated the piece of furniture which stood in one corner. 'Didn't you see me put them in there when we arrived? In any case, you probably wouldn't need them—you've been across into Vaud two or three times

since we came here without them. Of course, you could
wait until we return to Soleure, and then it would be
even easier.'

'What do you mean?' Mary asked.

'Bâle is still an open city, because it's partly in three
different countries. You have only to go there, cross the
Rhine bridge, and there you are in Baden, free to go
wherever you please. People who live or work there do it
constantly, and no-one attempts to check them because
it would be virtually impossible. Had you and your
friends gone straight to Bâle instead of entering Soleure,
you would have passed over into Baden quite easily.'

Mary recalled that someone had said much the same
when she first arrived in Soleure, but she had assumed
that she had misunderstood them.

'You wouldn't even need Captain Spengler's assistance,' Armand continued. 'Although no doubt he could
smooth your path for you, and there'd be advantages for
both of you. You go off with him and apply for an
annulment of our marriage, and he then reaps his reward
in the enjoyment of your—er—company.'

'I couldn't do that,' Mary replied soberly, without
even wondering why she couldn't. For all Captain
Spengler's noble profile and attentive manner, she
would rather stay here with Armand, cold, sarcastic,
disfigured though he was, and her life with him lonely
and a little frightening . . .

'You're afraid I'd pursue you for revenge, I suppose.
Well, I can only say that I've taken my revenge, and
whoever said that it's sweet was either a liar or a fool! I'd
rather you didn't go with him, but if you'd prefer to do
so, I'll not try to stop you.'

He spoke in the cold, even tones which were so much a
part of the wall behind which his feelings and character
remained hidden from her, but there was the slightest
hint of . . . what? . . . it was difficult to identify, for it

was so slight, but there was certainly some tiny nuance
in the tone in which he had said that he would rather
she didn't go, and Mary found herself replying firmly,
without hesitation or doubt, 'I don't wish to go with
him.'

'You're sure?'

'Yes.'

A quirk of the eyebrows, and then, 'Women are indeed mysterious creatures! I'm relieved to hear you say
it, for, firstly, he's already married, but lives apart from
his wife, and secondly, he's a Catholic, so will not be free
to remarry until she dies, and thirdly, you'd not be the
first unhappy wife he's run off with—not the second or
third! He pays them off well, when he's tired of them, I
believe.'

Silence fell, and dragged on for what seemed a long
time. Mary knew by now that Armand often used a long
silence for effect, but she was beginning to realise that
sometimes he merely refrained from speaking because
he had nothing to say, or perhaps because he preferred
not to say it, which was not at all the same thing. Nevertheless, something more needed to be said, so eventually
she asked, 'Are you angry?'

'With you? No, for you've behaved very properly,
although you must have been tempted. With him—yes.
Not for what he said about me, for that was true, but for
trading on your predicament for his own ends.' He spoke
slowly, choosing his words with care.

'Tempted?' Mary queried.

'He's a handsome fellow, rich, generous and kind—at
least as long as the liaison lasts, whereas I'm ugly, not
poor, certainly, but not wealthy either, far from generous in things which matter more than money, and extremely unkind. I can only assume that you regard a
contract as binding—even a forced one! Well, if you'll
excuse me—I must return to my duties, one mustn't

keep the Governor waiting—' and, with that, he heaved himself to his feet, made her a slight bow, and went out of the room.

Mary thought long and hard about the afternoon's events, particularly about her conversation with Armand, and came to the conclusion that she must have become fond of him, despite her frustrating inability to reach beyond his icy mask. If only he would thaw just a little towards her, make some small show of affection! It didn't seem possible that a man could make love as he did without some spark of tender feeling, yet he gave no sign of such feeling, still never spoke, however impassioned they became. That tiny, unidentifiable whatever-it-was in his voice when he said that he'd rather she didn't leave him was the only indication he had ever given of caring for her, and that was so tenuous that she thought now that she had probably imagined it.

She did not expect to encounter Captain Spengler again, and she was quite horrified when, only the next evening, she arrived with Armand to dine at a fine house in the Rue Calvin to find that he was one of the twenty or so guests. She saw him as soon as she entered the salon on Armand's arm, and tightened the grip of her fingers so convulsively that he made a faint murmur of protest. However, the Swiss kept his distance and acknowledged her presence with no more than a courteous bow, and she felt reassured that he had realised his mistake.

During dinner, he was seated some distance away, where she could not even see him, but after the meal all the guests adjourned to the salon and disposed themselves about the room in various groups. Mary fell into conversation with two ladies of her acquaintance and their husbands, both Army colleagues of Armand, who was sitting with a nearby group, listening to their talk, but, as usual, taking little part in it.

As she was talking, she became aware that another

person had joined them, and glanced up to see that it was Captain Spengler. She looked at him with disconcerted amazement, breaking off what she was saying in mid-sentence, and losing the thread completely, particularly as he began at once to behave in his usual attentive manner, which seemed utterly inappropriate under the circumstances.

She tried to edge away from him, unobtrusively shifting her chair, but her neighbour was too close for this to be very effective, and the result was only to allow Captain Spengler to move his chair more into the circle, and thus nearer to her, apparently under the impression that this was her intention.

'Dear lady!' he murmured under cover of a spirited discussion which had broken out between the others in the group. 'I'm sure that by now you will have seen the desirability of my suggestion!'

'No!' she replied, putting as much agitation into a low whisper as she could manage, and looking round des-pairingly for Armand. He was watching, and caught her eyes, holding them for a moment, then rose to his feet and strolled over in an unhurried manner to stand im-mediately behind her.

'Captain Spengler,' he said in a quiet, conversational tone. 'I thought my wife had made it quite plain to you that your attentions to her are unwelcome.'

'She has made it quite plain that she fears you beyond reason!' was the reply, but in a much more moderate volume than the Swiss normally employed. The conver-sation around them died away suddenly, and everyone in the group turned towards Mary and the two men. The sudden silence attracted attention from others as well, and soon most of the other guests were watching and listening.

Mary blushed, but spoke up bravely, and said flatly, 'That's not true!'

Captain Spengler stood up and glared at Armand, 'It's common knowledge how she was forced to marry you!' he said scornfully.

'And it's common knowledge that you're a skilled seducer of other men's wives,' Armand replied, sounding faintly bored. 'Although you failed to keep you own, I believe. Unfortunately for you, my wife prefers to remain with me, rather than depend on your uncertain protection.'

'A man like you could only get a wife by underhand means!' Spengler threw back in riposte.

'As you get your mistresses.'

'Jealous, are you? I've never had to force a woman into my bed!' Spengler jeered.

Armand propped his stick against the back of Mary's chair, and, without the slightest change in his unruffled expression, took off his glove in a deliberate fashion, and flicked Spengler in the face with it.

Mary felt sick, and the room swam round her. Dimly, she heard Spengler's request for the names of Armand's friends, and Armand's voice enquire of the two nearest officers if they would oblige, and then he drew her to her feet, and somehow apologies were made to their hostess who squeezed Mary's hands and seemed very concerned, and then Mary concentrated on making her legs carry her out to the carriage and the blessed darkness inside it.

'Oh, Armand . . . !' she faltered as the vehicle jerked into motion.

'I'd rather have avoided a meeting, but the fellow's become a nuisance,' was the only reply, and the rest of the short drive home was made in silence. It was not until they were home and in the sitting-room that either spoke again.

'What shall you do?' Mary asked unhappily.

'Do? Meet him, of course. You'd better take a glass of

brandy, I think. You look a trifle pale,' and with that, he went out of the room, returning a few minutes later with a glass already poured, and handed it to her as she sat huddled and wretched by the fireplace. She sipped it gingerly, and thought it tasted bitter.

'You mustn't worry,' he said in an unusually gentle tone. 'It's not your fault—you've behaved perfectly correctly. The whole trouble stems from Spengler's inordinate conceit—he can't believe that any woman who's taken his fancy could fail to succumb to his charms. I couldn't, in all honour, let the matter go on, and a meeting is the only way of stopping him.'

'But he might . . .' Mary tailed off, unable to finish the sentence.

'I shan't kill him. I'm a good shot, and I'll aim to miss. If I do wing him, I shall be more than surprised!'

This had not, in fact, been Mary's anxiety, and she thought that sufficiently important to try again. 'But he might . . . hit you!' which was still not quite what she meant.

'Possibly.' Armand gave his slight shrug, as if it were of no importance. 'If he does, perhaps you'll be free of me without the trouble of running off, or applying for an annulment. In that event, return to Soleure and go to General Eppler—he'll arrange matters for you. My will is in my office desk there.'

A tear trickled down Mary's cheek and gleamed in the candle-light as it fell. It landed on the skirt of her light blue silk gown and made a darker patch. Armand looked at it, frowned, and glanced at her face, then said, without any ironic inflection, 'It's unlikely. He hasn't any sort of reputation with a pistol.'

Mary surreptitiously wiped away some more tears under cover of pretending to rub her eyes, and drank the rest of her brandy as quickly as possible, as if it were medicine—indeed, it might as well have been, for she thought it tasted like a mixture of fire and wormwood.

'You'd better go to bed,' Armand said when she had finished it. 'I'll sleep in my dressing-room.'

'No!' Mary cried, then blushed. She was beginning to feel unaccountably drowsy, and not as much in control of her tongue as she would have wished.

'I shall have to wait up for my seconds,' he replied. 'There's no point in disturbing you once you're asleep.'

'I won't be . . .' Her eyelids dropped of their own volition, and her voice slurred. Armand drew her to her feet and guided her to the bedroom, where he rang for Irma. By the time she arrived, Mary was virtually asleep, sitting on the edge of the bed. Armand whispered something to Irma and then went out, leaving the maid to attend to her mistress, who murmured disjointly. 'Oh . . . I feel . . . Irma, I feel . . .' and then keeled over on to her side, fast asleep.

When she woke up, it was broad daylight. She felt bewildered, uncertain of her whereabouts at first, and her mouth felt dry and tasted unpleasant. It was several seconds before she remembered, and sat up with a gasp of horror. Armand was sitting on the stool before her dressing-table, tracing patterns on the carpet between his feet with his stick.

'It's all over,' he said matter-of-factly.

'What happened?' she asked, her face taut with anxiety as she looked at him for signs of a wound.

He stood up with an effort, as though he was very tired, and went to pull the bell which would summon Irma.

'I put a sleeping-draught in your brandy,' he said. 'It seemed the best thing. No point in you worrying—one way or the other.'

'And was everything . . . Oh, please tell me what happened!'

He gave her a curious look, and then said in the

tones of one telling a somewhat tedious tale, 'The agreement was one shot each. The seconds had to devise a different arrangement from the usual so many paces, turn and fire, because of this.' He gave his stick a slight jerk. 'So we stood two hundred paces apart, backs to each other, and turned at a signal. He was a good deal quicker at turning than I and got in first, but he missed, as I expected. Too much of a hurry, I think.'

'Missed?' Mary had an odd idea that he was lying.

He hesitated, then admitted reluctantly, 'The ball went through my sleeve and grazed my arm. Luckily, it was an old coat. I deloped.'

'Deloped?' The term was unknown to Mary.

'Fired in the air, it's an accepted way of indicating that one is satisfied with things as they are, when one's opponent has fired and missed. Otherwise, one would be virtually firing at an unarmed man, you see.'

'Yes.'

'Spengler has agreed to leave Genève immediately, and not to return while we're here. He still seemed to find it difficult to believe that you would really prefer my company to his, but he had the grace to apologise for his more personal remarks. I'm afraid you've wounded his vanity!'

There was a scratch at the door, and Irma entered with a tray bearing coffee-pot and cups. Mary drank hers gratefully, for the draught had left her mouth so very dry and she still felt heavy-eyed. After a slight hesitation, Armand also accepted a cup, and sat drinking it and looking rather abstracted as Irma bustled about getting Mary's clothes ready for her to put on.

'Irma, I think I'll wear the morning-dress with the lace flounce,' Mary said suddenly, knowing it was still downstairs in the ironing-room.

'I'll fetch it, Madame,' Irma replied, and went out.

Having made herself this opportunity, Mary said

firmly, 'I'll admit that I don't understand you, or know you to any great extent, and in some ways, you still frighten me a little, but I'd rather stay here with you than go with Captain Spengler, not because I'm afraid of what you might do, but of my own free will.' Her courage ran out at that point, and she waited uneasily for his reply, half-expecting something sarcastic.

It seemed a long time coming. He finished his coffee, got up and put the cup and dish back on the tray and stood looking at it for a moment, then moved across to the bed and took her right hand in his left and inspected it as if it were some interesting specimen. Then he raised it to his lips and kissed it, first the back and then the palm, closed her fingers over the kiss, and put the hand down carefully on the counterpane.

'Thank you,' he said, turned and limped quickly out of the room. He had not looked at her face once since she last spoke.

Mary sighed and wished most earnestly that she could gain some clue to his thoughts and feelings, and then wondered if perhaps he might say something later, when he had time to think about what she had said, but he made no reference to it at all.

Later in the day, Mary went alone to St Peter's Cathedral, feeling a need to give thanks for Armand's safety, and to think quietly about her situation. She knelt for some time in a side-chapel, and when she emerged into the body of the church, she was surprised to see Armand kneeling not far away, his face hidden in his hands. She drew back into the shadows as he raised his head, but his gaze was directed towards the east window, and she was able to slip past unseen, troubled by the unhappy expression on his face.

Life went on much as before, except that Captain Spengler was no longer there. No-one mentioned him, at least in Mary's presence, and nothing was said directly about the duel, although several ladies made a point of pressing her hand, or even kissing her, when they next encountered her, as if to express sympathy or approval, and Mary suddenly found herself treated as a friend by the same ladies who had sneered and criticised before. At first she regarded this change with mistrust, and then she realised that there was nothing hypocritical about it. Before the affair of Captain Spengler, she had been an outsider, an enemy, and now she had proved herself a loyal French wife, and she was accepted.

In spite of this change, she was greatly relieved when, a few days later, Armand said that they would be returning to Soleure at the end of the week. It was nearing mid-September now, but the weather continued hot, and, remembering how uncomfortable the heat had been on the last part of their journey here, Mary suggested that they make a very early start. Consequently, it was barely light when they set off. They reached Versoix as the sun rose and were able to admire the effect of the early sunshine on the distant snows of the Dents du Midi as a sleepy official waved them across the border without even asking for their papers.

The carriage was not swaying as much as it had on the outward journey as it had received some attention in Genève and the day was not yet really hot as they rolled along the lake-side road, so Mary was surprised when a sudden wave of nausea seized her.

'Oh!' she gasped, clapping a hand to her mouth. 'Oh, please—stop the coach! I—I feel sick!'

Irma at once began to exclaim and fuss, but Armand ordered the driver to stop, whisked Mary out of the vehicle, hurried her to the privacy of a clump of bushes by the road-side and stood by while she retched painfully a few times. Then he put an arm round her shoulders, smoothed her hair, and gently wiped her face with a clean handkerchief.

'I feel better now,' she said presently.

'You're sure?' he asked, looking intently at her face.

'Yes, thank you. It was most peculiar! Quite out of nowhere, I suddenly felt this awful nausea and cold sweat, and now it's gone again. Whatever can it be? Do you think I've taken a fever of some sort?'

'I'll send for the doctor when we reach Soleure to make sure, but I shouldn't think so,' he replied, his voice an odd mixture of sardonic amusement and hesitancy. 'I think it's more probably my fault!'

'Your fault?' she asked, puzzled.

'The result of our—activities—between the sheets, my dear! I suspect that you're with child!'

CHAPTER
EIGHT

THEY made an overnight stop in Avenches, and Mary was sick again in the morning. When they reached Soleure, Armand summoned the doctor, who confirmed Armand's suspicion, and seemed more exasperated than surprised that Mary's ignorance of her own bodily functions had allowed her to progress three months into pregnancy without realising what was happening. When he had gone, she sat for a while, looking unseeingly out of her bedroom window and thinking about her situation with a mixture of pleasure and apprehension, and then decided that she had better tell Armand what the doctor had said.

He was, as usual, sitting at his desk writing when she went into his office, for his *locum tenens* had already gone, apparently leaving a small mountain of problems behind him, but he put down his pen and rose as she entered, then stood looking at her with a slight frown as she said baldly, 'You were right. Dr Schmidt says we may expect the birth in April.'

Armand sighed, but all he said was, 'I see.'

'I—I thought you might be pleased . . .' Mary faltered, very close to tears at his apparent indifference.

'I shall be pleased when the child is safely born. You can't expect me to be thrown into ecstasies to hear that I've compounded my crimes against you by putting your life in jeopardy. Can you honestly say that, as things are, you're pleased yourself?'

'Yes. I want children,' Mary replied without hesitation. 'I'm only sorry that you don't share my pleasure.'

'I do,' he replied, looking away from her. 'At least, I

shall. When it's over and you and the child are safe, I'll rejoice as much as you could wish. Did the Herr Doktor recommend any particular course of action?'

'Only to avoid violent exercise and lifting heavy weights.'

'No more horse-riding, then.' He looked thoughtful for a moment, then went on, 'You'll need some new gowns, of course. For goodness' sake order them in something warm, not those flimsy muslins! It's very cold here in the winter. You may tell your dressmaker to send me the bills.'

The conversation virtually ended there, apart from a few polite exchanges, and Mary went away thinking what a strange man he was, to have married her by force, and yet to admit to feelings of guilt and anxiety because she was with child by him! He was generous with money, but she would rather he had given something of himself, some access to his mind and heart.

A day or two after their return to Soleure, Mme Eppler took Mary for a drive in her carriage and seized the opportunity of a private conversation to say that the affair of Captain Spengler was known in Soleure.

'I must say, my dear, how much I and all your friends sympathise with you in your predicament! I think you behaved splendidly!'

'Thank you,' Mary murmured, embarrassed.

'Things can't be easy for you,' Madame Eppler continued. 'A foreigner in a strange land, among people who must seem enemies to you, in view of all the circumstances, and your husband can't be an easy man to deal with. I mean no criticism of him, my dear! He's an admirable, an honourable man, but he's suffered a great deal, and he's been very lonely and withdrawn for many years because of his disfigurement and his lameness, both of which he feels acutely! I must admit that we were very surprised when he suddenly informed us that he was to be married, only the day before the ceremony, and then to someone he'd known such a short time! Some of our foolish young ladies with their romantic ideas called it a love-match, but I think otherwise—your face at the wedding was certainly not that of a girl in love!'

Mary opened her mouth to say something—anything —to stem this flood of speech, but nothing came, and she was forced to listen as it flowed on.

'Of course, there's nothing unusual in a woman being forced to marry a stranger, for one reason or another— why, I'd only met my dear husband three times before our marriage! It's a terrible shock, to find oneself sud-denly flung into bed, so to speak, with a strange man and his demands, but it's surprising how soon one becomes resigned to it, and, in time one grows fond of the man! Of course, children help—you'll find that when you have a baby or two to enjoy, you'll be much happier, you know!'

'I am quite happy,' Mary heard herself say in tones of great conviction. 'Armand—my husband—is very re-served, but he's kind and good, and I'm very fond of him, and I hope our first child will come in the Spring.'

Madame Eppler was delighted to hear it, and said so at great length. Mary was surprised at the ease with which she had uttered her convincing lie, but in the time she had for reflection while Madame Eppler's voice flowed on beside her, she decided that it must be the truth, to some extent, after all.

Her morning sickness recurred almost daily for a few weeks, and Armand seemed always at hand with the basin when she needed it, gently stroking her hair until it passed. Then it ceased, and she drifted into a placid, pleasant way of life, still going about visiting or shopping, still taking drives and gentle exercise, and feeling very well. She spent her time at home stitching baby-clothes and day-dreaming about the coming child, praying it might bring Armand out from behind his mask, as the brief autumn turned to winter, and the first snow came, thawed, came again, and stayed.

The new gowns came home from the dressmaker in good time for the colder weather. She had chosen fine cashmeres and merinos in rich shades of blue, green and dark red, lightened by contrasting braided trims, and fashioned into gowns with long sleeves and filled-in bodices. The fashionable high waist made them more comfortable and adaptable in wear as her figure changed, but she did not become nearly as large and unwieldy as she expected.

On the day that the first snow fell, she was standing at the dining-room window watching the falling flakes, when Armand came in for lunch with a dark object laid over his arm.

'I saw you go out with no more protection than a thin cloth redingote and a shawl yesterday,' he said, sounding distinctly disapproving. 'In future, until the warm weather comes, you are to wear this, and make sure you are warmly clad underneath it!' and he tossed his burden carelessly over the nearest chair.

'What is it?' Mary asked, and, as he did not reply, went to look. It was a hooded cloak, made to be reversible, with midnight blue velvet on one side and thick, soft sable fur on the other. It was so voluminous that she might easily have concealed quadruplets, or even another full-grown adult, inside it.

'Oh, it's beautiful!' she exclaimed, trying it on. 'How kind you are!'

'Kind?' He almost spat the word. 'That's not quite the epithet I would have expected! You'll wear it, or I shall beat you. Unmercifully!'

Mary laughed, and twirled before him, setting the cloak swirling out round her. She came to rest smiling up at him in an unconsciously coquettish manner, and surprised a distinct twitch in the muscle by his mouth.

'You're quite beautiful,' he remarked in an impersonal tone, much as he might have said 'It's snowing,' and rang for the servants to serve lunch.

As Christmas approached, Mary gave much thought to the choosing of gifts, and bought various things for Irma, Johann, the servants—even Sergeant Girard—out of what she had saved of her pin-money, and wondered what she could get for Armand. After much looking in shop-windows, and counting her money, she found herself at a loss, for she very much wished to purchase a handsome porcelain standish, complete with inkwell, sander, a box for wafers, pen-tray and taper-stick, glazed in dark blue livened with gold birds, laurel leaves and flowers, but it cost more than she had, even after searching her various reticules for odd coins.

She was seriously considering whether she had anything she might sell one morning as she lay in bed, waiting for Irma to bring the cup of chocolate which Armand insisted she must drink every morning before she got up, when he came in suddenly from his dressing-room and put a pile of coins on her dressing-table with an abrupt, 'I expect you wish to buy gifts for your friends, so you'd best have this. Let me know if you need more,' and went out again before she could thank him.

Consequently, on Christmas morning, she rose early in order to breakfast with him before going to church, and rather shyly put the wrapped and be-ribboned box containing her gift on the table at his elbow.

He looked at it in silence for a while, and then said, 'I thought it was customary to give presents to one's *friends*.'

'And family,' she added.

'I hadn't considered myself to be in either category.

However, I have something for you. You may exchange it if it's not to your taste,' and he produced a leather case from his pocket and placed it on the table in front of her, then gestured to her to open it.

The case was about eight inches long and perhaps four wide. It contained a chain and pendant of gold, set with a large oval topaz surrounded by smaller stones, each forming the centre of a gold flower.

'Oh, it's beautiful!' Mary exclaimed. 'Thank you!' She put it on and looked down at it, admiring the warm glow of the stones and the pretty setting, then smiled at him radiantly, thinking hopefully that he must care for her a little to give her such a lovely thing.

'I'm glad you like it,' he replied woodenly, and started to investigate his own parcel. When he had it undone and the pieces of the set unwrapped and assembled before him, he stared at them for so long that Mary thought that he disliked it. Then he shook his head and looked at her with a troubled expression and said, 'I didn't expect anything like this! It's exquisite, and I think that using it may almost reconcile me to my work! Thank you.'

Mary smiled at him again, trying to convey some of the warmth of feeling that she so much wished he would reciprocate, and she thought that, just for a moment, his calm expression softened, and a more human gleam appeared in his eye. Then he looked away and said, 'Oh, I'd almost forgotten in the excitement—I have something else for you,' and from another pocket, he produced a letter, which he handed to her.

It was addressed in a familiar hand, and Mary gave a little exclamation of pleasure and surprise.

'When did it come?' she asked, breaking the seal and opening the single sheet.

'Yesterday, but I kept it for today.'

The letter was from Lady Sarah. It said;

My dearest Mary,

We were both relieved and shocked by your letter, as you may imagine! We had been so worried about leaving you behind in Soleure, and dreaded that you might never be heard of again. In fact, we seriously talked of returning to fetch you several times on our journey. It was a relief beyond telling to hear from you and to know that you are not imprisoned, but the surprise of your news! We can only suppose that the terrible circumstances of our making the acquaintance of Captain Dufour must have given us a very false impression of his character, and we rejoice that you have found him to differ so much from the villain we thought him! We wish you truly happy, dear girl! and long for the end of this dreadful war so that we may all be reunited, and we may learn to know the true worth of the man you have chosen for your life's partner. Meanwhile, in view of the war, we think it best not to mention your marriage to anyone—I am sure you will understand. John encountered Mr Brown in London only last week, and did not even tell him of it, although he asked after you with great concern. John merely said to him that you are remaining in Soleure for the time being.

'It's from Lady Sarah,' Mary said when she had read it, and held it out to Armand.

'If I wished to censor your correspondence, I'd have done it before you read it, not after,' he said.

'She and Sir John send you their compliments. I don't mind you reading it,' Mary replied, but he shook his head.

'I would rather not. There may come a time when one of your letters contains something you would rather I didn't see, and then you'd be in a predicament.' He said drily, 'You must have told them something quite extra-

ordinary if they send me compliments and not curses!'
and with that, he abruptly excused himself, got up from
the table, and left the room, taking the standish with
him. In the doorway, he said, 'We'd best leave for
church in twenty minutes.' The letter was not mentioned
again.

The next time Mary went into his office, the standish
was in evidence on his desk, replacing the ugly stained
wooden one which he had used before, and he was
obviously using it, which pleased her very much, even
more than the possession of the topaz pendant.

After Christmas, both the winter and her pregnancy
began to drag on in a very tedious fashion. She felt very
well, apart from a tendency to tire easily, and was still
not so bulky that movement presented any problem, but
the cobbled streets were often slippery, and she was
afraid that she might fall, so she went out into the town
far less than before. The snow lay lightly on the countryside, far less heavy than in the Alpine region, and a little
more fell from time to time, but on most days, the sun
shone in a clear blue sky most of the day, and the air was
crisp and invigorating, making her long to be out and
about in it. However, it was very cold, and frequently
bands of fog would appear, without warning, lying like a
thick shroud over everything and blotting out any object
more than a few feet away, even in the town.

Armand bought a horse-drawn sleigh so that she could
still go out for drives, even after snow, but he instructed
her severely to wrap up well, and on no account to drive
herself, and she obeyed, but more from common-sense
that for any real fear of his severity.

She saw very little of him after mid-January, for there
was an epidemic outbreak of *la grippe*, which had started
in Paris and spread rapidly though France and her neigh-
bours, reaching Soleure at New Year. Most of Armand's
command of clerks and gate-guards succumbed, so that

he was very busy trying to keep things going, yet somehow he found time to order a cradle from the workshop of a craftsman of considerable local fame in the canton of Berne.

He said nothing about it, and Mary came upon it unexpectedly, standing in her bedroom, when she went up to change her clothes one afternoon. It was quite the most beautiful cradle she had ever imagined, let alone seen. It was suspended from a rail on a heavy stand, which would prevent it from overturning easily, and had a carved angel at the head and another at the foot, both with their hands raised in prayer, and their wings curving protectively until the tips of the longest feathers touched midway along the sides. The curved crib was strengthened by ribs carved with flowers, ribbons, fruit and birds in low relief, and on the underside of the stout bar from which the crib was suspended, where only the baby could see it, the figure of the Child Jesus was carved, his hand held up in blessing.

Mary went straight down to his office to thank him, and found him, as ever, writing a report of some kind. He listened to her thanks with a tired attention which was a trifle warmer than his usual cold courtesy, but only replied, 'I'm glad it's satisfactory,' and waited patiently for her to leave him to his work.

The epidemic continued into February, and it seemed that as one man returned to duty, another went down with the infection. The sick men were taken to the military hospital to be cared for, and the inn became very quiet and empty. Sometimes there was a man available to drive Mary's sledge, but she thought it best not to ask for one, but to leave it to whoever was in charge— which varied according to who was ill, Sergeant Girard having gone down with the infection at the end of January. On most days, she was not offered anyone, and had to be content to walk instead, venturing out if the streets

looked fairly free from ice, but more often tramping
briskly round and round the garden, even when it was
foggy.

One afternoon in mid-February, she was walking up
and down the paths in a patchy mist, Johann having
swept and sanded a route for her during the morning.
She was well-wrapped-up in her fur cloak and determined to walk for an hour and a half by the Cathderal
chimes, when, as she passed the little summerhouse, a
voice hissed 'Miss Burns!' from the dark interior.

'Who is it?' Mary spoke in English without thinking,
and peered cautiously into the little hut, poised to dart
away and shout for help.

'It's I, Roger Brown!'

'Mr Brown!' Mary exclaimed, looking towards the
inn, but it was only a looming presence in the thickening
mist. 'What on earth are you doing here?'

'I've been here for hours, in the hope of catching a
glimpse of you. I've come to rescue you!'

'Rescue me!' Mary exclaimed in consternation. 'But
how ever . . . Oh dear!'

She stepped inside the summerhouse, and asked
anxiously, 'But how did you know where to find me?
How did you get here?'

'Sir John told me you were still here, when I met him
in London during the autumn, so I determined to come
to your aid. It took me weeks to get a passage on a ship to
Norway, and then to one of the German ports, and then
to work my way south to Bâle. The chief trouble was
obtaining forged papers, both for myself and for you, for
obviously I couldn't risk entering French-controlled territory with English papers, and I assume yours have
been confiscated.'

'How did you enter Soleure?'

'Under a wagon-load of hay! I've been in the town
three days, making discreet enquiries among the towns-

people. I've been very careful to avoid the French, of course, so there was no great danger—obviously, the Swiss natives dislike the strangers in their midst!'

Mary thought he was wrong about that, but presumably no-one had told the French about him, or he would have been arrested by now. 'I'm not a prisoner,' she said, meaning to go on and explain the true position, but he interrupted, 'That will make matters easier, then! In fact, if you are not kept locked up, I marvel you have not escaped before, for I've always considered you a lady of courage and resource! It's one's duty to escape, of course, in order to prevent the enemy gaining any advantage from holding one prisoner, but I suppose it would be a little unreasonable to expect a lone and unprotected female to attempt such an adventure! However, have no fear, Miss Burns! I am here now, and I shall whisk you safely away from here, over the border, then take you home to your sorrowing friends!'

'I must tell you that I am married to Captain Dufour,' Mary said flatly.

The news was greeted with a gasp of horror. '*Married*? To that sarcastic, disfigured gargoyle? Oh, my *dear* Miss Burns! What you must have suffered! Oh, if only I could have come sooner! You must have no fear, however, I shall rescue you, just as I said, and I'm sure there will be no difficulty in your obtaining an annulment—any court in England would free you when the circumstances are known! We must go at once!'

'That's quite impossible!' Mary exclaimed. She wondered why people made such a fuss about Armand's disfigurement, as if that, in itself, disqualified him from any claim to be considered as a husband. She also wondered how she could break the news to Mr Brown that his noble and courageous rescue attempt had been a waste of what must have been an enormous effort for a man of his impractical and nervous nature. He would probably fly into the male equivalent of the vapours, so she deferred any mention of it until a more suitable opportunity in a less dangerous locality should present itself, and merely said, 'You must stay here for a while longer, while I think of a way to shelter and feed you for the night, and by morning, I must try to devise some means of conveying you safely away from here. Now, do not, on any account, step out of this summerhouse until I return, or send Irma, my maid, for you! If the fog lifts, you would be in full view of Ar . . . of Captain Dufour's window if you so much as show your nose outside! Stay here!' and she hastily walked away before he could reply, her mind in a whirl of plans and anxiety.

One thing she was perfectly sure about was that she could certainly not run off with Mr Brown and embark on a long journey to England when she was seven months pregnant, even if she wished to. For a few minutes, she allowed herself to think of the green, peaceful countryside of home, but found, to her surprise, that, much as she hoped to see it again, she was not prepared to abandon Armand in order to go there. In fact, the mere thought of leaving him made her feel quite ill!

What could she do, then? Tell him that Mr Brown was hiding in the summerhouse and shift the responsibility on to his shoulders? Hardly, for he could certainly do no other than intern Mr Brown, at least, and surely if he was found with false papers inside a garrison town, with no record of his legal entry into it, he was likely to be taken for a spy and . . . What would they do? Hang him or guillotine him? After all, he had come so far and taken that terrible risk in order to rescue her, so surely it was incumbent on her to rescue him in turn?

Somehow she must get him out of Soleure and set him on the road to Bâle, and persuade him to go without her. How?

After some twenty minutes or so of careful thought, she had a plan worked out, but its success or failure would depend on Irma, so, with some trepidation, she rang the bell for the maid, and waited nervously for her to appear.

'Are you not well, Madame?' Irma asked anxiously as she came in.

'Quite well, Irma, thank you, but something very unexpected and awkward has happened, and I need your help, if you'll give it me.'

'Of course, Madame.'

'Wait until you hear before you agree, for there may be danger in it. One of my acquaintances from England has come here under the mistaken idea that I'm in need of rescuing from the Captain!'

Irma gasped and put her hand over her mouth, her eyes two round circles of horror, or excitement.

'He smuggled himself into the town and has forged papers, so I'm afraid that, if the French catch him, they'll think he's a spy! Somehow, I must find shelter for him for the night, and food.'

'There's a dozen unused rooms in the inn,' Irma said at once. 'He could hide there easy as anything, and I could take him food while you're at dinner, ja?'

'Would you do that?'

'Yes, Madame.'

'Then tomorrow, if it's fine enough, I shall go out for a drive.'

'And hide him in the sledge?'

'No—better than that! He shall drive it! With Sergeant Girard ill, and some of the garrison men standing guard at the gates, they won't know he isn't one of the Captain's men—in any case, they hardly bother to look at my driver. Once they see my sledge, they're too busy opening the gates and standing to attention while I pass!

All they'll see is a man in uniform, and they'll assume he's one of our men.'

'Ah, *ja*—and I can get a uniform from the store! There's a great closetful of them in one of the rooms! How will you get back, though?'

'I'll take him towards Bâle, to a village where he can hire a horse, or a chaise, and then drive myself back.'

'I shall come too,' Irma offered, but she sounded less enthusiastic about that part of it, so Mary shook her head.

'No, better not, but thank you for offering. I don't wish to get you into trouble, and I shall have to tell the Captain what I've done when I return. Mr Brown will be safe by then, but I except he'll be angry, so it's best to keep your part as small as possible.'

Irma seemed quite happy, and, indeed, excited, about her part in the plot, which must have been a great event in her humdrum life, and even Mary's mention of possible trouble arising from it failed to dampen her enthusiasm. Mary told her where to find Mr Brown, and passed over to her the responsibility for smuggling him into the unused part of the inn, hiding and feeding him, and obtaining a French uniform for him.

At dinner, she was nervous and distracted, starting at every unexpected sound, and finding it difficult to make a convincing show of eating. Fortunately, there were no guests, and Armand was tired and preoccupied, hardly saying anything apart from a somewhat gloomy statement that, if the outbreak of *la grippe* did not soon pass, he would probably have to stand guard at all the town gates himself, simultaneously. He spent the rest of the evening trying to catch up on his reports, for several of the clerks had taken the sickness, giving him even more extra work to do. Mary offered to help him, and received one of his silent, unnerving stares in reply, followed by a faint smile and a grave little speech of thanks for her

generous offer, which was, however, declined, although
he added that he would bear it in mind, and might call on
her services if things did not soon improve.

Not surprisingly, Mary found sleep elusive that night.
She lay thinking about Mr Brown's unexpected arrival,
and marvelled that a man she had considered . . . well,
weak . . . should have found the courage to risk imprisonment or worse to come back into Europe and
travel all this way in an attempt to rescue her. He had
seemed so very frightened of internment, so concerned
about his own health, yet he had dared to travel with
forged papers, to hide for hours in a dilapidated summerhouse in the bitter cold, and all for nothing—unless
she went with him!

She toyed with the idea, but it was no more attractive
now than it had been earlier. Somehow, she had grown
too fond of her strange, reserved husband to wish to go
away from him, and the thought of life without him was
now not at all attractive. With a little sigh, she turned
towards him, and was surprised to hear him echo the
sigh.

'Did I wake you?' he asked.

'No. Is something wrong?'

A pause, then, 'Nothing of importance.'

'Can you not sleep?'

'No. This cold, damp weather makes my leg ache.' It
was merely a statement of fact, without any hint of
complaint or self-pity, but it was so unusual for him to
mention his disability in any but sardonic terms that
Mary put out a sympathetic hand to touch him. 'I'll go
into my dressing-room—I can toss about there without
disturbing you,' he said.

'I'm sure a cold bed would have an excellent effect on
your leg,' Mary replied in an echo of his usual ironic
tones. 'You're not disturbing me.'

He made no reply, but he stayed where he was, and

presently fell asleep, and Mary was not long in following.

The next morning was a nerve-wracking time and seemed to drag interminably, but Mary did not drive out in the mornings in winter, and dared not attract attention by doing anything unusual. She took lunch early, as Armand had gone out somewhere, and by two o'clock, she was well-wrapped-up in her voluminous cloak, clutching a hot brick over the bulge of her baby, waiting in the courtyard while Irma directed her 'soldier' driver how best to manoeuvre the sledge and its two horses out of the coach-house into the courtyard. There was no-one about, for only a dozen of Armand's men were not sick, and they were out on duty, and Johann and the servants were either taking their own meal or clearing up after it.

Mary settled herself into the sledge, and Irma tucked the rugs round her, making sure that they concealed the neat bundle which was Mr Brown's clothing and small valise. He was driving, dressed in French uniform, with a woollen scarf tied over his ears under his hat, and a fold of it swathed across the lower part of his face, so that, what with that and the low-pulled peak of his shako, only his nose was properly visible. Nevertheless, Mary prayed fervently that no-one from Armand's command would be on duty at the Bâle gate.

All went well. There were only two men at the gate, both from the main garrison, and they were busy collecting papers from the passengers on a mail-coach which had just arrived. One of them put up an officious hand to stop Mary's sledge, then hastily turned it into a salute and ran to open the gate for her, and stood rigidly to attention while the sledge slid and lurched past him, taking more notice of Mary's smile of acknowledgement than of the huddled wretch driving her.

The road was not particularly busy, but enough traffic used it every day to keep the snow down to a thin covering, even when they left the main route via Olten and turned on to a lesser road, which wound up a narrow valley into the Jura, and passed through two or three villages until it joined the main road again at Liestal. Mary had chosen it because any parties of French or Swiss soldiers who might be travelling would use the post road, and by coming this way, they would avoid the risk of encountering the military.

It was foggy among the hills, particularly in the side-valleys, which were full of grey mist, merging into white snow, and as they ascended on to the higher ground, it seemed to creep forward across the road, so that sometimes Mr Brown was only a ghostly shadow on the box in front of her.

Some two hours after they left Soleure, she called to him to stop. He checked the horses and drew in a little to the side of the road, then turned round and asked anxiously, 'What is it, Miss Burns? Is something amiss?'

'We must part here,' Mary replied. 'There's a village less than half a mile ahead, and I know you will be able to hire a horse, or even a chaise, at the inn there, to drive on to Bâle. You should have no problem at the frontier, for they take little notice of travellers crossing into Baden. You'd best change into your own clothes before you reach the village, or you may be thought a deserter. The inn-keeper is German-speaking, so you'll have no difficulty in dealing with him. Oh, and you'd best hide the uniform—bury it in the snow.'

'Part?' Mr Brown sounded astonished, which was not surprising. 'But you're coming with me! That's the whole point! You're coming back to England with me.'

Mary shook her head, 'No. I'm sorry. I'm married to Captain Dufour, as I told you, and I can't run away to England. I'm grateful to you for all you've risked and done in coming here, and I do wish that Sir John had told you the truth and saved you this long, difficult, dangerous journey. I am truly sorry, but I can't come with you.'

'But you can't wish to stay with that cold-blooded tyrant! The marriage can be annulled, I assure you . . . I'll set my lawyers to work on it as soon as we reach home!'

'No. I'm sorry,' Mary repeated.

'But why? I don't understand. Why?'

'I love my husband,' Mary replied firmly, voicing the fact for the first time, and knowing it to be true.

'*Love* him! A Frenchman? Good God! You can't *love* him! He's an enemy!'

'He is my husband, and I do love him!' Mary persisted.

'Then I wash my hands of you! I'll have no more to do with you!' He suddenly fumbled inside his greatcoat, and, after a struggle, produced a pocket pistol. 'Get down from the sledge!' he ordered, sounding petulant rather than threatening, and flourishing the weapon in a thoroughly dangerous fashion.

'But why?' Mary asked, shocked.

'You're a traitor! You meant to leave me on this road, then go back and set your husband's men after me! It's all perfectly plain now! Well, it won't work! You'll be the one left afoot, and I'll be in Bâle before you can get back to set the hounds after me!'

'Oh, you're wrong!' Mary protested, but he menaced her with the pistol and snarled, 'Oh, no I'm not! Unless they're already following . . . is that it? Well, if it is, I'll still give them a good run! Come, down with you, or I'll shoot you!' and Mary perforce disentangled herself from the rugs and descended to the roadway.

'You can't leave me here!' she cried, frightened now. 'I'm . . .' but before she could give the very good reason why he should not leave her, he cut in with, 'It's a bare half-mile to the village, so you say! I hope you fall in the ditch!' and with that childishly spiteful remark, he whipped up the horses and drove off into the fog. Mary called after him, but there was no reply, and the sounds of horses and sledge rapidly died away, leaving a dense silence.

Mary shivered. The fog was thicker and it was beginning to get dark early because of it. The sooner she reached the village, the better.

Wrapping her cloak round her, she set off along the road, but it was rough and rutted under the snow, and after a few yards, she tripped and fell full length, jarring all the breath out of her lungs, and lay still for some minutes, trying to summon the will-power to get up, and praying that she might not have harmed her child.

Presently, she got on to her hands and knees, and then to her feet, but, as she did so, a grumbling pain ran through her body, making her gasp and bend over. It lasted only a few seconds, then vanished. She put a hand to her brow, wondering if she had started to develop *la grippe*, but there was no sign of fever.

'Which way?' she thought, confused by her fall, and then stumbled along uphill, thinking that must be right, hardly able to see the road before her feet in the fog. The only way to keep to the road seemed to be to walk in one of the ruts, trudging along ankle-deep in the snow which filled it, but sometimes the road ran over rock and the rut petered out, and it was not always easy to pick it up again on the softer surface.

After some time, the same griping pain stabbed through her, and she had to stand still, half doubled-up with it, gasping, until once again it faded away.

'I must be ill,' she thought, for she was shivering as well now, yet her forehead still felt cool, which seemed odd if this was indeed *la grippe*. Whatever it was, she had to go on, so as soon as she could, she resumed her stumbling progress.

She had no idea afterwards of when and how she left

the road. It simply seemed to become rougher and steeper, and then the sloping ground on either side closed in and loomed out of the fog like walls, and she thought, in a vague, bewildered fashion, that she could not recall such a phenomenon from her drives along this route. It was not until she came upon a gate across her path that she realised that she had wandered off on to a farm track.

As she leaned against the gatepost, the pain came again, and she suddenly realised what it was—she might well have *la grippe*, but she was certainly in labour! No sense in trying to find her way back to the road—best go on to the farm, which must be somewhere ahead, and not, she hoped, too far!

On and on she went, tripping stumbling, trying not to fall for fear of harming the baby, stopping to huddle over her belly when the pains came, then struggling on through the darkness and silence, hardly aware of anything but the need to find help. Even a rumbling, crashing noise behind her, which grew to a crescendo that shook the ground under her feet, and then gradually died away, barely registered on her mind as she dragged herself along.

By now, the pains were coming much more frequently, and she was growing desperate, when suddenly a black shape loomed out of the fog and she came up against a vertical surface which was rough and hard against her hands. It took her a few seconds to realise that it was a plank wall, and several more to feel her way along it to a corner. A light gleamed faintly, seeming very distant, and she headed towards it, hands outstretched in front of her, until she reached another wall and found that the light came through a heart-shaped hole cut in a closed shutter. Near it was a door, and she pounded on it, crying out for help with all the strength she had left.

It opened suddenly, and she fell forward over the threshold into the arms of a stout matron of fifty or so, who appeared to Mary only as a cushioned body with strong arms, who half-carried her to a chair, keeping a continual string of exhortations and exclamations in German, punctuated by louder cries of 'Klara!' which Mary thought hazily were hardly necessary as the room seemed beautifully light and warm after the cold and darkness outside.

'My baby!' she gasped. '*Mein Kleinkind! Er komm!*' It was the best she could do, but the woman understood, for she pulled open Mary's concealing cloak and put a hand on her belly, just as another pain started.

Everything seemed to happen at once then. Mary was vaguely aware of someone else coming—a young woman with a baby in her arms, who put the child down in a cot and ran to help the woman—her mother? After that, there was the sound of the child crying, gentle hands helping her from the chair, supporting her, taking off her clothes, the two women speaking quietly and gently, their German seeming soft and unlike the usual harshly guttural sound of the language, and then the bliss of fresh sheets and lying down.

Then the pains really began, although at no time did they become as bad as Mary had imagined they would be. She heard herself crying out, calling for Armand, for she longed most desperately for him to be there, to help her through with this struggle. He, of all people, would know how to bear pain and overcome it. At one point, there was a pause in the battle to give birth, and she thought quite clearly that he did not even know where she was! Poor Irma would have to tell him about Mr Brown, and he would think she had run off with him. Then everything began again, and there was no time to think of anything but the need to push the baby out into the world.

By the time that the actual moment of birth came, she was so exhausted that she had only the faintest memory of it afterwards, no more than a climax of effort, and then a faint, reedy crying, which dwindled away into oblivion as she almost immediately fell asleep.

CHAPTER
NINE

She became vaguely aware of warmth and comfort, and of feeling curiously thin—not so much light in weight as less bulky. There was a pleasant smell of herbs—rosemary, she thought, and lavender, mixed with woodsmoke. Had Armand risen yet? She put out a hand towards him, and sighed when it encountered nothing but linen sheet, then opened her eyes.

The room was completely strange. It was small, with wood-panelled walls and simple wooden furniture—a table with a basin and ewer and a small mirror, a stool, a big chest, and a cradle. Even the bed was a plain wooden one.

'Oh!' she exclaimed aloud, and sat up, her hands going to her body as she realised what had happened. She was quite flat—the rounded bulge of the baby no longer there, and she was wearing a coarse linen nightshift.

'Good morning!' said a pleasant female voice in German, and Mary turned her head towards the door and stared blankly at the young woman who stood there. She seemed vaguely familiar, and the name Klara slipped into Mary's mind.

'Where am I?' she asked.

'This is my man's father's farm. You came out of the night, lost in the fog—not last night, but the one before —with your baby coming. You've been asleep ever since he was born.'

'He? A boy?' Klara nodded. 'Where—is he—all right?'

'Quite all right. Rather small, but he was early, perhaps?'

'Yes. I thought another two months . . .' Mary looked
eagerly towards the cradle, and Klara went to it, lifted
out a bundle in a white shawl, and brought it over,
putting it carefully in Mary's arms. A crumpled red face
was framed in the woollen folds, with a thatch of black
hair.

'He's beautiful!' said Mary entranced, and the baby
opened his eyes, smacked his lips, and scowled, then
began to cry. It was quite a lusty noise, much louder than
Mary expected.

'He sucks well!' Klara observed. 'I've been feeding
him with mine, to save waking you. You must have been
very tired. Had you come far?'

'I got lost on the road from Soleure to Bâle,' Mary
replied, giving the baby her breast in an awkward, half-
frightened way. Klara leaned over and helped her.

'Your first, isn't it? I've had two before, but they died.
The one I've got now is all right, but a girl. Better luck
next time, I hope! You weren't walking, were you?'

'Someone stole my sledge and horses,' Mary replied.
It sounded very unlikely, but Klara seemed more interested in the baby. 'Then I wandered off the road somehow, in the fog. My husband doesn't know where I am!
Is there anyone who could go to Soleure and tell him?'

'Oh, dear!' Klara bit her lip and frowned. 'No, there
isn't. The father is old and lame, and the mother's feet
are bad, and I can't leave the baby. My husband's in the
Army, and the boy's gone to Bâle—he won't be back for
a day or two. Anyway, the track's blocked. There was a
bad rock-fall in the narrow part, where it passes between
the crags. You must have passed it just before it came
down—lucky you weren't a few minutes later!'

Mary had a hazy memory of the rumbling, crashing
sound which had shaken the ground—so that was what it
was!

'Is there no other way out? No-one who lives near

and could take a message? I can pay . . .'

Klara shook her head. 'No, I'm sorry. There's no other farm near, and we can't get the cart out to the road to go to the nearest place. As soon as Piet comes back from Bâle, we'll send him. He's not very bright, but he's reliable, and you can trust him to take a message,' and Mary had to be content with that.

The next day, she ventured out of bed on very wobbly legs, but by the day after, she felt well enough to dress and sit in the farm kitchen, where the old man made polite conversation with her between lengthy periods of dozing, and the old woman gave her a great deal of sensible, peasant advice about babies, cooking, milking cows, concocting remedies for various ailments, brewing potions, averting the evil eye and raising chickens, between giving her three substantial meals during the day and standing over her while she ate them. Klara showed her how to change the baby, lending her the necessary cloths, as she had already lent garments and a shawl from her store. She also showed her how to bring up the baby's wind, and all the other things she needed to know to look after her child. The girl seemed amused that Mary knew nothing about it, but was sympathetic when she explained that her own mother had died when she was a child, and she had never known anyone with a young baby who might have taught her such things.

At last, on the fifth day, the boy Piet returned. He came into the kitchen in the early evening, put down the large covered basket he was carrying, and sat down on a stool before the stove to pull off his heavy boots without saying a word, his rather vacant eyes looking at Mary in a faintly puzzled fashion. Then, having set the boots side-by-side in the chimney-corner, he pulled off his knitted cap, revealing a shock of fair hair, and gave her a little bobbing bow and a slow smile.

'This is Piet,' said Klara. 'He's my husband's little

brother. He's simple and shy, but quite harmless. We'll teach him your message, and tomorrow he can go to Soleure and find your man, and tell him where you are.'

'Perhaps it would be better if I wrote a letter,' Mary said, thinking that more obvious and practical than trying to teach the boy something parrot-fashion, for he might forget, or tell it wrongly.

'Letter?' Klara sounded surprised. 'I thought you must be a lady, with that lovely cloak and your beautiful clothes and all! None of us can write, nor read, so we've no paper or ink or pens. Piet will be all right—he's always taking messages—quite complicated ones—and he gets them right.'

So Mary carefully explained to Klara who Armand was, and where he could be found, and kept her message to the very simple statement that she was well and would the Captain please send a carriage to fetch her.

'Oh, but what about the avalanche?' she interrupted herself.

Klara questioned Piet about it, phrasing her enquiries so that his answers were little more than 'Yes' or 'No', and it emerged that it was possible to get past the fall on foot without much trouble, and he was sure the lady could do so if she was helped, giving Mary his sweet, vacant smile.

In the morning, he recited his instructions and the message without the slightest hesitation or mistake, and seemed to understand exactly what he had to do. Mary gave him the pass which Armand had written for her when he first gave her permission to go out of Soleure, thinking it would help Piet gain access to Armand more quickly. The boy took a cloth-wrapped bundle of bread and cheese and set off, plodding away across the yard in his heavy boots. Mary watched until he disappeared round a curve of the track as it entered the narrow valley, and then she sat down to nurse her baby and wait.

She was amazed by the perfection of the child. Her fall on the road had not harmed him in any way, although she supposed it must have brought on his premature birth. He was a little small, she thought, but was not sure, never having seen so young a child before. His hands and feet were beautifully formed, and he seemed to have the right number of everything, and to be very active, waving his limbs about a great deal and making little crowing noises when he was not asleep. He seemed to sleep a lot, but Klara said that was quite normal, and, indeed, her own child, who was three months old, slept quite as much. When he needed to be changed, or was hungry, his voice was surprisingly powerful, and so was his suck and his appetite. He seemed to have grown and filled out already, and no longer looked so crumpled.

Piet returned in the early afternoon of the next day, accompanied by Sergeant Girard, who took one look at Mary, standing with her child in her arms and smiling in greeting, and exclaimed, 'Oh, God be thanked, Madame! We've been worried out of our minds, and we hardly dared believe the boy! He just kept saying the same thing over and over, and we couldn't get any more out of him! You really are all right. Madame? and . . . and . . . ?' he gestured towards the baby.

'Perfectly all right, thanks to these good people. You brought a carriage?'

'We brought your sledge, but we had to leave it down the track, for there's a great fall of rock across the way. The men are trying to clear it, but can you walk so far?'

'I think so.'

The conversation had been in French, but Klara seemed to have caught the gist of it, for she told Piet to go and harness the horse to the little cart, and fetched Mary her cloak and bonnet.

'You'll eat something before you go?' she asked the Sergeant in halting French, but he declined, thanking her, but saying that his men were waiting, and the Captain too.

'He's with the sledge?' Mary asked. She had hoped that he might have come for her, but, of course, he could not climb over a rock fall and walk along the rough track to get here.

'No, Madame,' Sergeant Girard said reluctantly. 'He —wasn't able to come. He wanted to, but he's been ill . . . nothing to worry about, but he couldn't come out . . . doctor's orders.' Mary was disappointed, but assumed that he must have come down with *la grippe.*

She tried to give Klara's mother-in-law (whose name she had never discovered) some money, but the old woman was only persuaded with difficulty to accept a ridiculously small amount, and Mary could only get Klara to take a few coins by saying that they were for her child, and even then, Klara insisted that she must keep the shawl and the few clothes she had borrowed for the baby. The old mother gave both Mary and the baby a lengthy blessing, and a jar of ointment to put on him if he was at all sore, and then Mary climbed into the cart and set off for home, with Piet leading the horse and Sergeant Girard walking beside him, and Mary's new friends waving farewell from the farmhouse door.

The journey back to Soleure was uneventful, once Mary had been helped over the rock-fall by two strong soldiers, who virtually passed her from hand to hand. Sergeant Girard carried the baby, and was distinctly heard to make chirruping noises and tell it what a fine little man it was. Some of the soldiers stayed to help Piet clear the track, and the rest mounted their horses (very clumsily in some cases, as they were all infantrymen) and escorted Mary's sledge. She expressed surprise to Sergeant Girard on seeing it, but he said in a very matter-of-fact way that the person who had borrowed it sent it back from Bâle, and she thought it best to save her questions for Armand.

Her entry into Soleure was almost a triumphal progress, for the guards at the gate greeted her with beaming smiles and words of welcome, and several of her acquaintances waved or bowed to her as she went by. She was pleased to see that enough of Armand's men had, like the Sergeant, recovered from their illness and returned to duty.

At the inn, Johann and a tearful Irma came running out to greet her, but no Armand. Irma said nervously 'Oh, Madame! I had to tell him everything when you didn't come back! I didn't know what else to do! I told him I was sure you meant to return, but I don't think he believed it, for he didn't do anything until he got the letter . . .'

'Letter?' Mary asked, puzzled.

'I don't know what it was, or who from, but a man brought it, and your sledge and horses, and after that, he was out every day from first light until late at night, searching, and a lot of the soldiers with him. He was frantic!'

'Was he angry with you?'

'No. He just thanked me for telling him.'

'Where is he?' Mary was bitterly disappointed that there was no sign of him.

'In his office. He . . . he's not well . . .' Irma looked anxious, yet seemed reluctant to say more, so Mary did not press her. She surrendered her cloak and bonnet to the maid, let both her and Johann see the baby, then arranged her shawl to help support him, and walked a little hesitantly along the passage.

The office seemed empty when she entered, and almost in darkness, for the daylight was fading outside and no candles had been brought. The only light came from the log-fire, which threw confusing shadows. Then she saw that Armand was standing by the window, once more a darker shadow against a dark velvet curtain.

'Marie?' he said, sounding unusually hesitant and uncertain.

'Yes,' She moved a little towards him, but he remained quite still, half-turned away from her, so, with sinking spirits, she sat down on the sofa, the baby cradled in her arms, fast asleep.

'I'm sorry,' she began after a few seconds of silence, during which Armand hardly stirred a muscle. 'It should have been a simple matter of an afternoon drive, but it went wrong.'

'So I gather. I assumed you'd gone with him, until a man brought back the sledge and a letter. It was addressed to you, but I took the liberty of opening it.'

'From Mr Brown?'

'Yes. It's here, somewhere.' He gestured vaguely towards the desk, but made no move to find it. 'He apologised for abandoning you on the road—he said he was so shocked and horrified by what you said, and your refusal to go with him after all the trouble he'd taken, that his anger overcame his good sense!' His calm voice broke suddenly, and he sounded anguished as he burst out, 'My God! Didn't he know you were with child?'

'No,' Mary replied, wishing he would at least look at her. 'He only saw me for a few minutes in the garden, and then in the sledge, and I had on my big fur cloak. He wouldn't have realised, and I didn't tell him. How did you know about him before the letter came?'

Armand gave a mirthless grunt of laughter. 'He was seen about the town, pretending to be in disguise! Half a dozen people reported his presence to me, before he ever managed to contact you!'

'And you didn't arrest him?'

'How could I? For one thing, he's a timid fellow, yet he found the courage to come back into the dragon's den to try to rescue his princess! I must admit that the English—even the most rabbit-like of them, can find great courage at times! For another thing, I thought you—cared for him.'

Mary stared at him, confused and very puzzled, and presently he went on, 'It seemed one solution to the problem. He'd look after you, and probably marry you after the annulment, if you went with him. I thought it best to leave the decision to you. Why didn't you go with him? He didn't say in the letter.'

'I didn't want to.' Mary could not quite bring herself to the point of telling him exactly why, for he seemed so distant and cold, almost as if he would have preferred her to have gone with Mr Brown. 'He was very angry, and called me a traitor for choosing to stay with you. He made me get down from the sledge because he thought I meant to come back and send your men after him during the time it would take him to walk into the village and hire a horse to go on to Bâle. I meant all along just to get him safely out of Soleure and set him on his way, and then drive myself back home in time for dinner. I felt that I had to help him escape, as he'd come here on my behalf, and I was afraid that, if he was caught, he might be shot or hanged as a spy.'

'Very likely,' Armand confirmed grimly. 'Yes, I can quite well understand why you had to help him—I'd have done the same in your place—but for him to leave you on the road . . .!'

'It was only half a mile or so to the village, and ordinarily it would have been nothing. I could have walked that far without any difficulty, but the fog came down, and somehow I wandered off the road, and the . . . the baby started to come . . .'

Armand rubbed a hand over his face, as if he were very weary, and said in a raw, uneven voice, 'At least, you survived. We searched every possible road, not knowing which one you took. I remember the track, but when we came to the rock-fall, we didn't go beyond it. Well, I suppose it's no use indulging in a mass of regrets and "if onlys". We must think of the future now.' He paused, and seemed to gather his strength in some way before continuing, 'I'll give you a sworn statement that I forced you to marry me against your will, and there'll be no problem about the annulment of the marriage. Then I'll arrange for you to go home to England. It'll mean a long journey, but not too difficult or dangerous.'

Mary was so shocked at his apparent dismissal of her as his wife that she was unable to speak.

'It doesn't set matters right, of course,' he went on. 'I can't give you back your virginity, or undo all that you've suffered because of me. I only wish I could! I knew I was hopelessly wrong from the moment it was too late to go back! I must have been mad to think that there could be any satisfaction in trying to take revenge by hurting you, just because you happened to look a little like the woman who injured me! In fact, I was so deranged that I couldn't even recognise the real reason why I was marrying you until it was too late!'

'What was that?' Mary asked.

'I—wanted you, for yourself, not for revenge, or . . .' he broke off and shook his head. 'What does it matter? I've ruined your life, and all I can do is set you free to try to find some sort of happiness. For what little it's worth, I'm sorry.'

He was silent again. The fire crackled and Mary sat numbly trying to make sense of what he had said and trying not to cry. Then she said hesitantly, 'What about the baby?'

'The baby?' He jerked as if she had struck him.

'Am I to take him with me, or will you keep him? I suppose he'll be illegitimate . . .' She broke off, unable to continue.

'But the boy said . . . the simple lad from the farm . . . all he would say about the baby was that it came too soon. I thought he meant that you'd . . . lost it . . .'

'It was less than two months too soon! That's why he's rather small, but he's strong and healthy, and feeding well. I suppose you didn't ask poor Piet any more, and he was too simple to add anything. He can't cope with anything but plain questions and "yes" or "no" answers.'

'Where . . . where is he?' Armand asked harshly.

'Why, here! Come and see him!'

If he'll only come and look at him! Mary thought. *Surely he won't send me away when he's seen his son!* She sat up expectantly as Armand moved towards her, and watched in puzzled amazement as he walked straight into his desk, catching himself a painful knock on the thigh on the edge of it, and her amazement turned to horror as he felt his way round the corner and moved forward again, only to collide with a chair which was in his way. His left hand groped until it found and gripped the chair back, and then he came on, feeling his way with his stick, his other hand outstretched, ready to fend off any more obstructions.

'What is it?' she demanded. 'Can't you see?'

'I'm blind,' he replied curtly as she reached up to guide him to a seat on the sofa. 'Not permanently, I think, but totally, for the time being.'

'What happened?'

'I spent three days out on the roads, with the sun glaring on the snow. It often happens—it's called snow-blindness. Normally, it passes after a few days, but with me—you remember, you said I shouldn't work so much by candle-light? It seems that I've over-strained my eye for a long time. The doctor says that I shall probably recover a little sight, enough to walk about without knocking into the furniture, but not to read or write. At least, I'll get my discharge from the army, so I can go home and do something more worthwhile!'

'Oh, Armand!' Mary put her hand on his, where it rested idly on his thigh, and, after a few moments, he turned his hand up to grip it.

'The baby?' he asked. 'You said it's a boy?'

'Here he is.' Mary carefully laid the baby in the crook of Armand's left arm, then guided his right hand to touch the little face. He gently traced the child's features, and then suddenly cried out, 'Oh, God help me! What am I to do?' in tones of such anguish that Mary gasped in consternation.

'I thought you'd lost him, you see,' he went on in a lifeless, wretched voice. 'I hoped, when you were carrying him, that I might find some way of breaking down the wall between us, but I couldn't—it just seemed to grow worse. During these past few days, searching for you, then sitting here with nothing to do but think, I thought I'd driven you away to hide, or . . . When the boy came and said you were safe, I made up my mind that I must do what I could, though it's ridiculously small, and set you free. But now . . . if I free you, I make a bastard of an innocent, helpless child . . . my son . . . !'

He must have made some sudden convulsive movement, for the baby opened his eyes and began to cry, a protesting little sound at first, but soon swelling into a thorough lusty keening. Armand turned helplessly to Mary and said anxiously, 'What is it? What's wrong?'

'He's hungry, and I expect he needs to be changed,' Mary replied calmly, taking the squalling bundle. 'I must take him upstairs and see to him, and then I'll come back and we'll talk properly.'

Armand nodded, but made no other reply. He seemed to be straining to see her as she left the room.

'It will be all right,' she said, turning in the doorway, but he did not appear to hear her.

Feeding and changing the child, then settling him to sleep in his beautiful cradle, watched over by the two hovering carved angels and, more actively, by Irma, took quite half an hour, and then Mary left them and went downstairs.

At the bottom of the flight, she sat down on a step and made herself think calmly about the possible courses of action open to her. Knowing her own weakness, she must be very careful not to let her imagination mislead her, so she had to take stock of each step in her reasoning for possible error.

Well, now—she could accept Armand's suggested solution, regardless of his concern about the child, and apply for an annulment of her marriage, which would allow her to return to England, either leaving the baby with Armand, or taking him with her. Could she do that?

The answer was 'no', whichever way she considered it. She could not abandon her child, and, despite the fact that she would have enough income to support him, and no doubt could pass as a widow at home, she knew now that she had no wish to leave Armand, and he was quite as important to her as the child. She had loved him without understanding him, despite his mask of indifference, but now she knew it was only a mask, for had he not said that he had wanted to break down the wall between them? Surely that was evidence of some feeling for her, and, added to that, he had said that his real reason for marrying her was that he 'wanted' her, whatever that might mean—well, there was only one way to find out! She would have to ask, and go at least halfway to meeting him over this wall-breaking business.

Why had he appeared almost anxious to be rid of her? It must be because of his guilty feelings over the way he had forced her to marry him, and if he thought that she didn't care for him . . . After all, she had done very little to demonstrate her affection, so he must think that she hadn't any!

She thought back over some of the things he had said at various times, and began to find a coherent picture emerging, a portrait of a man who was sensitive, and therefore likely to be very conscious of his disfigurement and lameness—he had made jibing references to them several times. Perhaps it had never occurred to him that she might have grown to love him, in spite of everything, for, after all, she found it quite surprising herself!

So there was her course of action—to ask Armand what he meant by 'wanting' her, and to tell him that she loved him and had no wish to leave him. She stood up, took a deep and steadying breath, and marched herself back into his office.

Someone had brought candles and drawn the curtains, but Armand still sat on the sofa, as she had left him, his head bent and his hands clasped on the handle of his stick. It seemed very odd to see him sitting idle, and he had what struck Mary as an attitude of patient hopelessness. He lifted his head and turned his face towards her as she entered, and again asked 'Marie?' in that hesitant, uncertain manner.

'Yes,' she replied, and went to him, sitting close by his side and putting her arms round him.

'There's no need to pity me,' he said coldly. 'I shall see again, in time, and this serves one good purpose, by getting me my discharge.'

'Why do you want to be rid of me?' she asked quietly, without moving away or releasing him.

'I don't. Your freedom is all I can give you.'

'But I could have taken that, by going with Mr Brown.'

'Why didn't you go? You said you didn't want to, but that's not much of a reason.'

'Why did you marry me?' Mary countered. 'You said

just now that it was because you wanted me, but that's not much of a reason either.'

He was silent for so long that Mary thought he was not going to answer, but eventually he said reluctantly, 'I suppose—oh, it's no use talking about it! I'm disfigured, maimed, and now blind! I assume that you felt obliged to stay with me, either out of pity, or respect for a legal contract. I'm grateful to you, but I can't accept your pity, and a forced contract isn't binding in law, so you're not obliged to stay.'

'Don't you think it's time we started telling one another the truth?' Mary said quietly but firmly. 'That wall you spoke of is built of evasions and concealments. If you really wish to break it down, start by answering my question, and then I'll answer yours.'

Again he was silent, and then, in a taut, harsh voice, said abruptly, 'I love you.'

'And that's why you married me?'

'I didn't realise it at the time, not until after I'd forced myself on you, but yes, that's the real reason why I married you.'

Mary relaxed now, certain of her path and what she must say.

'And the reason why I didn't want to go with Mr Brown is because I love you, and have done so for months, although I was even slower to realise it than you! I've been so blind, and with less excuse than you have!'

The last sentence came into her mind as a flash of inspiration, and somehow she had time to consider it and decide in favour of saying it without any hesitation becoming discernible in her speech. She knew she was taking a risk, for he might well take it for a cruel jibe, but it appealed to his sardonic humour and he laughed, a genuine sound of amusement.

'Did you tell Mr Brown that?' he asked.

'Yes. He was very annoyed!'

'I should think so! Imagine St George coming to fight the dragon, and after all his trouble, the princess says she likes the dragon better than the saint! Mortifying!'

'Armand,' Mary began, speaking on impulse again, but on a subject that had occurred to her before. 'I know marriage is only a civil contract here, but do you think we might be married again in church? I don't know what the words are in your sort of service, but in England, husband and wife promise to take one another "for richer, for poorer, for better, for worse, in sickness and in health," and that's how I would like it to be for us.'

'Yes, I should like that very much,' he replied. 'Marie, does it seem to you that we've been a pair of fools? I could have come to you months ago and said "I'm sorry I forced you to marry me. I love you", but I was afraid to try it!'

'I could equally well have admitted that I loved you,' Mary replied. 'I didn't at first, of course! You frightened me, made me feel uneasy—do you remember those interviews? I couldn't read your face at all, and your manner was so cold and intimidating! Then, when you told me what had happened to you, I was sorry for you, but frightened for myself . . .' She shook her head, remembering her confusion and perplexity. 'And you seemed like two different people! During the day, you were cold and sarcastic and shut away from me, but at night you were gentle and tender, yet you hardly ever spoke . . . I was so confused!'

'When did you start to love me?' he asked.

'I don't really know. My—my body loved you first, almost at once—after a week or so—but my mind and heart . . .' She paused, thinking back. 'I think it must have been when we went to Genève.'

'And I thought you were falling in love with Spengler!'

'I didn't really like him very much,' Mary replied

candidly, and believed it to be true. 'But he was the only person there who was kind to me, you see, and you were so busy and tired, and seemed to have lost interest in me. I'd never had so much attention from a handsome man before—oh, except Mr Brown, of course! I suppose I was flattered and dazzled . . . At least he made me realise where my affections were really fixed!'

Amand put his arms round her and sought her face with his lips, arriving first at her cheek, but soon finding his way to her mouth, and kissed her properly for the first time, opening up a whole universe of new delights to her which she had never dreamed might be contained in so small a concept as a kiss.

Some time later, he said rather shakily, 'Marie, what is the baby called? You haven't told me his name.'

'He hasn't one yet. I thought you would wish to choose it.'

'But you must have some preference.'

'Only for whatever you choose.'

'Is that the truth?'

'Of course. I'll choose the names for our girls, and you for our boys!'

He laughed again, and seemed to be getting more used to doing it. 'If we'd had any sense, we might have discussed this months ago! Well, then—I suggest we call him Jean. It sounds much the same in English or French, and it will remind us of your kind friend, Sir John Robbins. Also, it was my father's name.'

'Jean Dufour,' Mary tried it out. 'Yes, that sounds very fine and proper!'

'Marie,' he said again, after another interval. 'After all I've done to you, the way I've treated you, it's hard to believe that you love me—no, I don't mean that, for you've had two, no, three, opportunities to leave me, but I've treated you cruelly, I'm ugly, I'm French —if you stay with me, you may not see your home again for years! How can you bear it?'

'Well,' Mary considered the matter, 'I'll agree that there are some drawbacks to loving you, but, on the other hand, there are some compensations. I think that, on the whole, the compensations must carry the day!'

'And the drawbacks?'

'I shall just have to make the best of them! After all, you can't help being French, can you?'

He laughed, then became serious again. 'This war may drag on for years, Marie. I could arrange for you to go to England, but not both of us. If you stay with me, you'll be cut off from your friends, your home, but I promise you that when the war ends, I'll take you back to England. It's the best I can do.'

'If it lasts too long, there may not be any reason for me to go back at all,' Mary replied soberly. 'Sir John and Lady Sarah are my only real friends there, and they're no longer young . . .'

'But you must have other friends?' Armand sounded puzzled. 'And surely you've had other admirers than Spengler and Brown? Did you live in some inaccessible fortress in England?'

'Very nearly!' Mary replied. 'Broadwood Magna isn't very far from London, but the road to it doesn't go anywhere else, you see, so it's never been turnpiked, and it's well-nigh impassable half the year, and muddy and rutted all the time, so no-one ever goes there! That's why my father chose to live there, I suppose. He was very unhappy when Mother died, and wanted to shut himself away from everyone.'

'Broadwood Magna,' Armand made a creditable attempt at the name. 'Tell me about it.'

'It's just one street,' Mary began, settling comfortably in the curve of his arm and smiling a little in reminiscence. 'It starts at the top of a hill with the church and a black and white rectory, and then the cottages tumble

down the slope, like children's toys, until the street ends
by the duck-pond—or in it when it rains! There's an inn
called the Green Dragon by the pond, where George
keeps his ferrets—do you remember? All the village
men gather there in the evenings and drink ale and
gossip, like old women!'

'And where do you live?' Armand asked, his voice
muffled because he was kissing Mary's hair.

'In a brick house, half-way down the street. It's the
only one, so it's called Brick House, and opposite are the
gates to Broadwood Manor, where Sir John and Lady
Sarah live.'

'Are there no other gentry in the village?'

'No, nor for some distance round about, so I'd never
been in Society until we came to France. I used to
daydream about it . . . In fact, I wasted hours imagining
what might happen, and never did anything to help it
happen!'

'What did you imagine?'

'Oh, silly things, like some handsome gentleman accidentally riding through the village and falling in love
with the pretty girl in the garden—and never stopped to
think that I was weeding the path with an old dinner-
knife, with mud on my face and my hair in a bird's-nest,
and an apron over an old, old frock, looking anything
but pretty! In any case, why should a gentleman be
riding by? He'd have had difficulty finding Broadwood
on purpose, let alone by accident! Do you know, when
we came to France, I imagined myself meeting a tall,
dark, handsome Frenchman who would beg me to marry
him and heal the breach between our nations . . . What a
foolish, nonsensical child I was!'

'Marie,' said Armand softly. 'I love you very much.
Shall we heal the breach between our nations for ourselves, and hope that our governments will have the
sense to do the same before long? I'm tall and dark and

French, which is three-quarters of what you imagined! I should like to see your Broadwood Magna and your Brick House. What will those gossips in the Green Dragon say when you bring home such a battered, ugly, *French* husband?'

Mary hesitated, wondering herself what they would say, and then she remembered a conversation she had once heard.

'There's an old man called Garge in Broadwood,' she said at length. 'He's been claiming he's past ninety ever since his sixtieth brithday, which was four or five years ago, and he rules Broadwood Magna! He tells everyone what they should think, what they should do, and they always do as he says! Now, he says that all gentry are foreigners, because we all came over with William the Conqueror, or Dutch Billy, or German George, so he'll say that you're no more foreign than I am, only my family's been in England a bit longer, that's all! Only the labouring people are really English, according to him, and what the gentry do doesn't signify in the least because we're *all* foreigners! Then he'll tell them all to shut their mouths and drink their ale, and that'll be the end of the discussion!'

'And your friends, Sir John and Lady Sarah? What will they think?'

'As long as I'm happy, they'll be content,' Mary replied. 'And Lady Sarah will be delighted if we've several children—four or five, at least!'

'Well, we've made a start towards delighting her!' Armand said, smiling. His voice was warm and alive now, having quite lost its old dry, cool tones. 'Oh, Marie! An hour or two ago, I was sitting at that desk in the depths of despair, with all my life in ruins! I saw myself going home to the Gironde, alone in the dark and wretched, to live out my life in bitter loneliness and regret! I never dreamed that everything could change in so short a time! I think it's almost more than I can bear, to go so suddenly from the very nadir of despair to such a height of happiness! Will you come home with me, Marie, or would you prefer that I sell my land and buy an estate somewhere else, on neutral ground—in Switzerland, perhaps?'

Mary half-consciously noted that he had said 'Switzerland' quite naturally instead of the usual sardonic 'Helvetic Confederation', and smiled as she replied, 'Oh, if you're willing to live in England some of the time, when we can, then I'll be content to live in France! As long as I'm with you, I don't care where we are!' and she raised a radiant face to receive and return his kisses.

Sergeant Girard, who had quietly opened the door, closed it again, and went off rubbing his hands with satisfaction to tell Johann to delay dinner at least another hour.

Masquerade
Historical Romances

Intrigue excitement romance

Don't miss
February's
other enthralling Historical Romance title

KING'S PURITAN
by Jean Evans

The year is 1651 and England's only hope for the future lies in
Charles Stuart's escape to France from Cromwell's rule.
To Verity Ashbourne, a secret follower of the King, the
advent of Richard Kingston, the commander of a troop of
Roundheads billeted on her home, is a continuing threat to that
hope and to those of all royalists. How can she remain silent
when she suspects him of being a spy? Yet any other time but this
she might have loved such a man . . . She despises all he stands
for, so why does her heart play the traitor?

**You can obtain this title today from your local paperback
retailer**

Masquerade
Historical Romances

Intrigue excitement romance

THE GOLDEN BRIDE
by Ann Edgeworth

When Lalia Darrencourt, heiress and acknowledged Victorian beauty, is jilted by her fiancé a week before her wedding she is convinced she wants nothing more to do with love, but when she discovers her mistake it is almost too late . . .

PRINCE OF DECEPTION
by Valentina Luellen

On her arrival in St Petersburg, Emma Fraser is horrified to find that the man she took to be a fellow servant is Prince Michael, head of the House of Adashev. How can she trust him when he has already deceived her once – especially when he seems to be so closely involved with the Czarina Catherine.

Look out for these titles in your local paperback shop from 12th March 1982